"WHAT ARE YOU DOING HERE?"

"Looking for you," said Didi Nightingale. The seat next to him was taken, so she slid along the bar and stood next to him.

"No cows in Philly," he noted.

"I don't want to make small talk with you, Detective Pratt. It was too hard finding you. Besides, we really don't like each other."

"I'll buy that," Pratt retorted. "Can I buy you a drink before you leave?"

"No. And I'd prefer you left with me."

"Is this a proposition?" Pratt asked.

"Sure," Didi replied bitterly. "I want to seduce you so you can write me a love letter."

"Weird sense of humor you have."

"Take a ride with me, Detective. A nice long ride to Hillsbrook. I want to prove that what you think and what is the case are two different things. I want to present you with the corpses and the murderers."

Pratt laughed. He was beginning to enjoy the repartee. He wondered whether he should tell this arrogant young lady that there was yet another corpse. . . .

THE DR. NIGHTINGALE MYSTERY SERIES
BY LYDIA ADAMSON

Dr. Nightingale Chases Three Little Pigs

A DEIRDRE QUINN NIGHTINGALE MYSTERY

Lydia Adamson

A SIGNET BOOK

SIGNET
Published by the Penguin Group
Penguin Books USA Inc., 375 Hudson Street,
New York, New York 10014, U.S.A.
Penguin Books Ltd, 27 Wrights Lane,
London W8 5TZ England
Penguin Books Australia Ltd, Ringwood,
Victoria, Australia
Penguin Books Canada Ltd, 10 Alcorn Avenue,
Toronto, Ontario, Canada M4V 3B2
Penguin Books (N.Z.) Ltd, 182-190 Wairau Road,
Auckland 10, New Zealand

Penguin Books Ltd, Registered Offices:
Harmondsworth, Middlesex, England

First published by Signet, an imprint of Dutton Signet,
a division of Penguin Books USA Inc.

First Printing, August, 1996
10 9 8 7 6 5 4 3 2 1

Chapter 1

Deirdre Quinn Nightingale, D.V.M., ripped off her examining gloves, rolled them into a ball, and flung them into the bucket.

"Well?" Lou Tisdale's question came out as an aggressive bark.

Didi didn't answer. She stepped away from the cow she had just examined and studied her.

The patient was a lovely little milk cow with very large ears.

But she had stopped eating, her milk production had declined, and her bones were turning brittle. She moved ever so slowly, getting up and down with tremendous effort.

Oh, yes . . . this lady . . . and in fact her name was Lady . . . was a sick cow.

There were five other cows in the barn. Didi walked past them one by one. They seemed fine. Their breath was like steam in the freezing barn.

5

"I know what's the matter!" Lou Tisdale fairly shouted.

Charlie Gravis, Didi's geriatric veterinary assistant, couldn't let that pass. He retorted angrily: "If you knew what's the matter, why the hell did you get an old man like me out of a warm house on a day like this?"

"Who wanted you!" Lou snarled. "I wanted her! She's the vet. If you knew anything about cows, Charlie, you'd still be a dairy farmer."

Didi stepped between them before it escalated further.

"Gentlemen, please! Let's deal with the matter at hand." She was used to defusing situations involving angry dairy farmers. These days, they were always angry. Milk prices kept going down. Feed prices kept going up. The squeeze seemed eternal.

Then she smiled in an almost daughterly fashion, and asked, "What is the matter with Lady, Lou?"

"Radiation," said the farmer. Then he took off his wool hat, shook it, and replaced it on his balding heat in a different position.

Charlie Gravis guffawed. Didi signaled to him that he should keep his mouth shut.

She moved her toes furiously in her boots; the cold was numbing them. Lady started to bellow weakly and roll her eyes. There was no steam coming from her muzzle now.

"What do you mean—'radiation'?" Didi asked Lou.

"I mean that damn nuclear plant on the Hudson. Their poison is leaching into the wells. And I'm going to sue them."

Didi pulled her ski hat down further on her head but it couldn't cover her exposed neck. I should let my hair grow out in the winter, she thought.

Then she silently walked over to Lady and looked her over once more, feeling the front legs and shoulders.

She stepped back. "Tell me, Lou, what do you feed your herd?"

"The usual. Dried forage."

"Baled?"

"Yeah."

"Off the trucks?"

"Right."

Didi nodded. All year long, huge flatbed trucks came into Dutchess County from Canada and the Midwest, selling baled hay and other forage at discount prices. Dairy farmers and horse breeders depended on them.

"What kinds of grains do you feed them?"

"None."

"None? How about protein supplements?"

"None."

7

"What about bonemeal or wheat bran or soybean meal?"

"No."

"Are you serious, Lou?"

Lou Tisdale didn't answer.

"Answer the doctor!" Charlie demanded.

Lou was silent.

Didi walked up to him. She spoke slowly and forcefully. "I don't think it's radiation poisoning, Lou. I think it's phosphorus deficiency. A vet doesn't see it so often anymore. Know why, Lou? Because every dairy farmer has been sent hundreds of notices over the years by county agents, farmer associations, and veterinary groups, warning against feeding dairy cows just dried forage. You have to supplement the diet because the forage is marginal in phosphorus content."

The big dairy farmer thrust out his gnarled hands in a pathetic gesture.

"The wife works part-time in town," he said, "and I haul trash three times a week. Just to make ends meet. I can't feed any other way."

"Then you don't belong in this business anymore," Didi said. And a moment later she felt ashamed of herself for the comment.

"Can't you just give her an injection?" Lou pleaded.

"No. It's chancy. Excess phosphorus is even

worse than a deficiency. Get some bonemeal, Lou. Or wheat bran—that's even better. Do it now, Lou."

Didi and Charlie headed for the red Jeep.

He climbed into the passenger seat and dumped the bag into the back.

Didi went around the front of the vehicle. She was so cold and angry that she didn't even notice the vehicle parked near hers.

But then she heard: "Dr. Nightingale, I presume."

She wheeled and stared at the kindly old mustachioed face in the open car window.

"Hiram! Hiram!" she yelled, and rushed over to his car. She stuck her head in through the window and kissed her old professor.

Then she stepped back. "I can't believe it's you," she said, laughing.

"Well, it is," he replied.

Didi just stared at him happily, lovingly. Hiram Bechtold had been her favorite professor at the University of Pennsylvania School of Veterinary Medicine. He was the best . . . the smartest . . . the most kindly. He had retired from full-time teaching after she graduated, to "think," as he put it. Didi had kept in touch with him by phone, had asked him for help in diagnosis and treatment, but she hadn't seen him in almost five years.

"Well, follow me home, Hiram! I want you to see the house and the clinic and meet my elves."

He held up his hand.

"I can't, Didi. I have to get back. It's a long drive home. But I did get to see your house and meet your Mrs. Tunney. She was the one who told me you were here."

Didi was confused. Why had he made the long drive up, just to turn around and go back?

Hiram picked up on her confusion. "I did come here to see you, Didi. But it isn't a social call."

"What, then?"

"Clifford Stuckie was murdered in Philadelphia two nights ago. Horribly murdered."

At first, the name didn't ring a bell. But then she remembered. "You mean, *the* Clifford Stuckie, Hiram? The millionaire? The one who owns Rising Moon Farm, here in Hillsbrook?"

"And, Didi, a beef cattle operation in the Florida Panhandle, plus homes in New York and Colorado and God knows where else. Yes, Didi, that's the one."

"I didn't see anything in the Hillsbrook paper."

"It was all over the Philadelphia papers. But I learned it from a police officer. They came to my house five hours after the murder."

"Your house? Why?"

"It seems his Rolodex in the carriage house where

he was murdered was open to my name and number."

"Did you know him?"

"No, not really. Of course I knew *of* him. But I spoke to him only once, a few years ago. He told me he had an experimental hog-breeding place in Hillsbrook, that he needed a good vet, and he asked if you were reliable. I told him you were the best."

"They do call me every few months. And they do pay their bills on time."

"The police found something else in the carriage house, Didi: a love letter."

"Well," she said, "he does have a girlfriend. I met her once at Rising Moon."

"It was written to you, Didi," Hiram announced.

Didi was stunned.

"To me! Are you serious?"

"Yes."

"But I barely knew the man, Hiram. I met him briefly, maybe three times over the years. When I go there, I deal mostly with the foreman. I forget his name."

Bechtold didn't speak for a long time. He stared through the window at Lou Tisdale's crumbling barn.

"Are you okay, Hiram?" Didi asked.

"Didi," he said, "they think—they think you may be involved in the murder. Do you understand?

They consider you a suspect in Stuckie's murder. They're coming here, to Hillsbrook."

"Hiram! What are you saying?"

"They think you may have killed him. Because of the letter."

"My God. You don't believe that . . . do you, Hiram?"

"Didi, I'm an old man. I don't know what to believe anymore."

"Hiram, this is me! This is your old student. Didi Nightingale. I'm a country vet, remember?"

But the old professor had rolled up the window.

He started the engine and drove off without saying another word.

Didi watched him go. The darkness was coming. She looked into the red Jeep. Charlie was dozing.

What is going on? she thought. What madness is this?

The wind was flaring up. But she didn't move.

Something was nagging at her, making her very uncomfortable.

When he had refused her offer of hospitality, she had wondered why he would make the long drive just to turn around and go back.

Now she wondered why he'd made the trip at all.

Why *had* Hiram Bechtold driven all the way from Philadelphia in the dead of winter to tell her this strange tale?

Why hadn't he just picked up the phone?

That would have been the rational thing to do.

Didi looked at old Charlie Gravis dozing in the Jeep.

Hiram was even older than Charlie, and feebler.

What if the whole outlandish story was just a figment of an aging man's deranged imagination?

Alzheimer's? Senility? Severe depression?

Yes, she thought, it was probably that. One of those. Her eyes welled up with tears. Poor Hiram! The moment she got home she would have to call his wife, who was probably worried sick over her wandering husband.

Didi climbed into the Jeep.

"Do me a favor, Charlie. First take me home. Then take the Jeep to the post office before it closes and check for mail. I'm expecting a lab report."

By the time they arrived home, it was pitch-dark.

She waited until Charlie drove off and then headed toward the house.

"Didi!"

"Who's that?" Didi asked, peering at the two figures who were suddenly visible on her right.

"Allie."

"Oh, Allie. You scared me. How are you?"

Allie Voegler was, as usual, underdressed. No coat. Only a muffler hanging loose over his red flannel shirt. He looked very big in the darkness.

"I'm fine, Didi. I want you to meet someone."

Didi laughed and said, a bit flirtatiously, "You sound very serious, Allie. Are you trying to fix me up?"

Allie don't laugh. The stranger next to him was still silent.

"Didi, this is Detective John Paul Pratt, of the Philadelphia Police Department. He wants to question you."

The stranger took a step forward and thrust out his hand for Didi to shake.

Didi kept her hands by her side.

She didn't feel like being friendly or hospitable.

All she felt was an inexplicable dread. As if she were a child again, lost in the pine forest as darkness closed in.

Chapter 2

Didi didn't like the looks of the man—this John Paul Pratt. He was short and burly and looked constricted in his three-piece black suit and white shirt.

His eyes were strangely opalescent, like those of freshly killed trout.

"Well, I'm finally in your bedroom," Allie quipped with an exaggerated leer.

"First and last time," Didi muttered angrily. Allie gave her a hurt look.

Pratt seemed to ignore the bantering. He was seated on one of her mother's rockers.

Allie sat on the other and Didi sat on the bed.

A bedroom was no place to conduct business of any kind. She should have taken them to the clinic office or the living room, or even the kitchen.

But Didi had the feeling this John Paul Pratt should be kept away from her elves.

A burst of cold wind battered the window panes. Didi gripped the sides of the bed.

The police officer from Philadelphia pulled an object from his black attaché case and placed it on the small table between the two rockers.

Didi stared at the object. It was familiar.

When she realized it was a tape recorder—that she was about to be interrogated—she exploded, rising up off the edge of the bed.

"Are you serious! This is the most ridiculous thing I have ever heard of. Just an hour ago an old friend told me I was a suspect in Clifford Stuckie's murder. Something about a love note. I thought he was crazy. Now I can see you are all crazy!"

"Relax, Didi," Allie said. "He just wants to ask you a few questions."

"And what kind of friend are you?" Didi asked bitterly, as if Allie Voegler should protect her from these ridiculous intrusions.

"I'm a police officer, Didi. I'm performing a professional courtesy for a police officer from another jurisdiction. That's all."

Didi sat back down. She folded her hands in her lap. It was best, she realized, just to get this stupid thing over with.

John Paul Pratt switched the recording device on.

"Are you aware that Clifford Stuckie was murdered in Philadelphia two nights ago?"

"Yes," she replied.

"How did you become aware of that fact?"

"I told you. An old friend came to see me. He told me."

"What is his name?"

"Hiram Bechtold. He was a professor at the University of Pennsylvania School of Veterinary Medicine."

"Did you attend that school?"

"Yes."

"Did he tell you the cause of Mr. Stuckie's death?"

"No. He just said it wasn't pretty." Didi could see Allie Voegler squirm.

"Do you know Junior Walls?"

"I've never heard the name before."

"Do you know Pilar Walls?"

"No."

"Did you ever visit Clifford Stuckie's carriage house in Philadelphia?"

"No."

"When was the last time you were in Philadelphia?"

"Years ago."

"Can you be precise?"

"Three years ago."

"Can you account for your whereabouts the last three days?"

"Of course I can."

"And nights?"

"Of course. I've slept in this room for the past three nights—and a couple of thousand nights before that. I go to sleep about eleven. I get up at five-thirty. I go out into the yard and do yoga. And there are four people who live in this house with me who can confirm that."

"What are their names?"

"Mrs. Tunney, Charlie Gravis, Trent Tucker, and Abigail."

"Are they relatives?"

"No."

"Employees?"

"Sort of."

Detective Pratt shut off his machine and began to rummage in his case.

"Well, Officer Voegler," Didi asked sardonically, "should I get a lawyer?"

Allie didn't respond. Detective Pratt pulled out some papers. He crossed the room and handed her a two-page, poorly reproduced typescript. At the top of the first page was STATEMENT OF JUNIOR WALLS.

"Would you please read this," Pratt said, and returned to his rocker.

Didi read it carefully:

My name is Junior Walls. My wife's name is Pilar. I am a jazz pianist. She is an ethnomusicologist. We are both graduate students at Temple University.

We both occupy, rent-free, the second floor of Clifford Stuckie's carriage house in return for custodial services.

Mr. Stuckie comes and goes as he pleases but he rarely sleeps there more than twice a month. Mr. Stuckie usually arrived at odd hours.

On the night of February 3, a noise from downstairs woke me at approximately two a.m. At first I could not tell if it was Mr. Stuckie. There was a lot of rain and wind outside. Then I heard the phone closet open and I knew it had to be him. He had installed a phone jack in the closet and kept it under lock and key.

I went back to sleep.

At around three a.m. Pilar woke me. She told me she smelled something funny. We went downstairs and found the body. There was blood all over.

I dialed 911 and waited. We didn't touch anything, but we threw one of the blankets over him.

Didi looked up, signaling that she was through.

Pratt crossed the room, took the statement, and handed her another document.

"Now I'd like you to read portions of my report."

This one had been reproduced on a better machine, although several passages had been blacked out, purposefully.

Didi read:

I arrived at the carriage house at 3:22. I removed a blanket from the body. Stuckie was lying facedown on the floor. He wore pants but no shoes, socks, or shirt. His arms were tied behind his back, at the wrists.

There was no sign of struggle. There was no sign of forced entry.

The chest area was covered with matted blood.

The caretakers reported no shouts or screams . . . no signs of even an argument . . . no sounds that would point to another individual in the carriage house with Stuckie.

The wounds were shallow puncture type. Perhaps made by some kind of ice-pick-type instrument. It appeared that Stuckie had bled to death.

The body lay five feet from an open phone closet. The telephone had been brought out into the room. The wires were clearly visible. The phone rested on the floor, on a small, folded-up rug, halfway between the open closet and the body. Next to the phone was an open Rolodex.

Didi stopped reading for a moment. She remembered that Hiram had told her the Rolodex was open to his name. Then she continued reading:

A restored antique carriage took up about a third of the floor space. On the carriage seat I observed several objects.

I identified a fine-line Magic Marker, an old-fashioned wood chess board, obviously used to write on, a brief note written in what I assume to be the victim's hand, and a stamped, addressed envelope.

All the rest of the report was blacked out.

Detective Pratt took the document back and handed her a single sheet of paper.

"This is a photostat of the envelope found at the crime scene."

Didi took it and stared. The envelope had her name and address clearly written on it. But it seemed unreal to her.

"Look," she said, holding the paper, "it wouldn't have been delivered anyway. That's a twenty-nine-cent buffalo soldier stamp. First-class postage is thirty-two cents."

Pratt ignored her comment. He took the paper back and handed her another sheet.

"This is the note found at the crime scene," he declared.

There was a knock at the door.

"Yes?" Didi called out.

Mrs. Tunney walked in, carrying three mugs of her famous cocoa on a tray. Didi grimaced. She hadn't asked Mrs. Tunney for refreshments, but she should have been able to predict that the old house-keeper would appear. Didi was behind closed doors with two men in her bedroom. Of course the suspicious Mrs. Tunney would find a way into that room. She had to see what was going on.

Mrs. Tunney set the cups down, gave Allie Voegler a dirty look, gave Detective Pratt an angry one, and said to Didi: "I'll be downstairs, dear, if you need me."

"Thank you, Mrs. Tunney."

The old woman left. No one touched the cocoa. Didi read the letter:

> *Dear D: If you knew me well, you would loathe me. But only for a while. Love redeems. And my love for you is so fierce it could catapult a million sinners into paradise.*

She placed the paper down on the bed and leaned back. She felt suddenly very tired and very confused. She didn't know what to say.

Detective Pratt retrieved the paper, went back to the rocker, and switched the recorder back on.

"Were you and Clifford Stuckie lovers?" he asked.

"No."

"You never slept with him?"

"No."

"Did you date him?"

"No."

"Did he ever tell you he loved you or desired you?"

"No."

"But you did know him, didn't you?"

"Barely. I met him two or three times."

"And he never even hinted that he was in love with you?"

"Never."

"Did he ever send you flowers?"

"No."

"Any gifts?"

"No."

"Where did the two or three meetings take place?"

"At Rising Moon Farm."

"What were you doing there?"

"I'm a veterinarian. They called me for help in farrowing."

"What does that mean?"

"I'm there when a sow has a difficult birth. I clip and tie the navel cord of each piglet. Then I shear off the needle teeth. Then I notch the ears to identify each pig in each litter. And I come back five days later to castrate the boars."

Didi vaguely heard Detective Pratt ask her another question. But she ignored it. She stared down at the muted design of her mother's quilt on her mother's bed in what had been her mother's room.

23

What could have been in that strange man's head to send her such a letter?

It was unbelievable. She couldn't even remember what he looked like. All she could call up from memory was a lithe blond man who wore boots and was always pleasant. She couldn't even remember his face.

Didi folded and unfolded her arms nervously. Had Clifford Stuckie been following her, watching her, stalking her—without her knowing it? She shivered a bit.

Men, she knew, found her attractive. She was pretty by popular standards. But men also found her rather dull, she had learned, because she was so absorbed by her work.

No one had written her a love letter since she was in sixth grade. This one from Clifford Stuckie, it went without saying, was infinitely stranger than the heartfelt, misspelled epistle from little Tommy Hawes.

Didi looked suddenly at Allie Voegler and said, "You never sent me a love letter."

The moment she said it, she regretted it. Allie flushed and squirmed. She realized he had not told the detective from Philadelphia about their "special relationship"—whatever that meant.

"I would have if it would have helped my

chances," he replied. And then he added, bitterness in his words, "Besides, I'm not rich or handsome."

"Or dead," she muttered.

"Is there anything else you would like to say at this time?" Detective Pratt asked her.

Didi didn't like the tone of the question. It implied she was hiding something. Now she was convinced that she had been right to dislike this visitor on first sight.

"Well," she said softly, "yes, there is something I would like to say."

Detective Pratt clasped his hands and leaned forward expectantly.

"You're going to have a serious case of dandruff on your hands if you don't do something soon."

Pratt glared at Didi. Allie rolled his eyes in exasperation. Pratt snapped off his recording device and took a sip of the cocoa. He pushed it away immediately.

Then he stood up. "We will be speaking again, Dr. Nightingale," he said.

That was meant to sound like a threat, Didi supposed; it was meant to unnerve her.

And it did.

There was no package—no mail at all—for Didi Nightingale, D.V.M., at the post office.

But Charlie did not mind making the trip into town—because it was a Lotto night.

And the winning New York State Lotto ticket in this evening's game would be worth a cool 11,500,000 dollars.

The first thing I will buy when I win, thought Charlie Gravis, is a red Buick.

He stood on the dark main street contemplating the lines of the vehicle. He had seven dollars to bet on the Lotto. That meant fourteen games . . . fourteen sequences of six numbers each.

Charlie wasn't really a gambling man. But now he had no options. His desire to make millions by marketing his revolutionary herbal treatment for canine lumbago and other disorders had been brutally thwarted. Not by the blind forces of the marketplace or the power of the pharmaceutical companies. Oh, no. By those closest and dearest to him. By Mrs. Tunney and Trent Tucker and Abigail. They had simply disallowed it on the grounds that Dr. Nightingale would have kicked them all out of her house if she discovered such an enterprise operating on her poor dead mother's property.

Cowards all, Charlie thought.

He reached into his back pocket and brought out the seven Lotto cards, held together by a clip, along with the seven dollar bills.

Then Charlie marched toward Hudson Stationery, the new store in Hillsbrook that sold greeting cards, paper goods, paperbacks, magazines, newspapers, assorted gums and candies, cigarettes, and lottery tickets.

He usually purchased his Lotto tickets on the highway. This was the first time he had ever set foot in the stationer's.

And the moment he did step inside, he was greeted with, "Fancy meeting you here, Charlie Gravis."

He couldn't place the plump woman who had greeted him from behind the counter. Charlie looked at her, puzzled.

"Ben Harrah's daughter," the woman reminded him, picking up on his perplexity. "Toby. I'm Toby Harrah."

"Hello!" Charlie gave an exaggerated greeting to make up for his memory loss. Ben Harrah had been a friend—and a fellow dairy farmer, whose spread was just three miles outside of Hillsbrook. But he was long dead.

Charlie thrust the tickets into Toby's hand. She in turn slid them effortlessly into the Lotto computer.

"Hope you got a winner, Charlie," she said cheerfully.

Charlie thanked her. But in truth he felt no confidence at all in his selections. He had used his normal selection process: taking down the numbers from the first license plates he could read in the morning, then putting them on slips of paper, shaking them up in a hat, and pulling out six at a time.

Toby handed Charlie the computer tickets. He handed her the seven dollars.

He started toward the door but stopped when he heard laughter at the back of the store. He peered along the brightly lit aisle.

A man and a woman were standing in front of a magazine rack. The woman held an open magazine. They were both laughing at something in the magazine.

Charlie realized the woman was Didi's friend Rose Vigdor. The Nature Girl. The handsome young blond woman from New York City who had come to Hillsbrook to live in an old barn with no electricity or running water—and three dogs.

He didn't recognize the thirtysomething man.

Their laughter came in waves now. It was obvious they were having a fine old time.

"Who is that with Miss Vigdor—her beau?" Charlie asked the counterwoman.

"Goodness, no. That's Ed Newman. He comes in here most every evening for something. Or just to look."

"Is he from Hillsbrook?"

28

"He just moved here. A nice man. He teaches math and computers at the high school."

Her voice lowered. "They say he's very smart."

"They used to say that about me, too," Charlie quipped.

He put on his spectacles and started down the aisle. The teacher was well-dressed. He was about middle height and extremely thin. His face was narrow and dark. When he laughed he folded his arms. He looked lonely, Charlie decided.

Charlie walked outside and lit a stub of a cigar, shielding the match expertly against the wind with his gnarled old hands.

He could feel the lottery tickets in his pocket. All eleven million dollars' worth. He laughed at himself. He never got more than two numbers right out of six on all the tickets he had purchased over the years.

That never used to bother him. But now it did. Now he had to win something big. And fast. Time was short. He felt it.

Turning away from the wind, he stared through the store window. The two magazine browsers had separated, each to his own interest.

He could see this Ed Newman clearly.

He wondered if the teacher played the Pick-Six Lotto. Probably not. What a shame! Everyone knew that the only way to win was to use a computer to create a betting strategy. To identify, isolate, and predict "hot" numbers. Charlie had read all about this and he believed it. Yup, that was the only way to go.

Charlie stamped his feet. He was freezing. He had to get back home.

But he kept staring through the window, watching Ed Newman.

An idea began to come to Charlie Gravis. It was a rather devious idea—maybe even a wild idea—but, after all, the stakes were very high. It was worth the risk.

Chapter 3

Didi eased herself into the lotus position on the frozen ground just behind the large house.

It was six-fifteen in the morning, the sky still dark.

Mrs. Tunney had just turned on the kitchen light and was starting to prepare her blasted oatmeal.

The cold was excruciating. Didi wore fur-lined boots, gloves, a ski parka, and a face mask.

She started her breathing exercises. The steam from her breath was white and beautiful. But the actual inhalation and exhalation were painful. It was simply too cold for any form of outdoor spiritual questing in Dutchess County, New York.

For Didi, however, these exercises were a matter—and a test—of faith. She had vowed to do them each morning even if a hurricane was blowing. And she kept her vows.

She began the second phase of the exercise—

holding one's breath and counting silently, then, very slowly, releasing that breath as if it were the most treasured of substances.

The purpose of the yoga was to cleanse and still the mind . . . to remove all dross and anxieties . . . to prepare for the day.

But this morning the measured breathing techniques merely intensified her memories of the previous day and that unsettling, inexplicable love letter.

Poor man!

Why was her mind fixed on the letter? Clearly, she should be thinking of the man, not the aberrant letter . . . thinking of a brutally murdered human being with a family, with friends, with aspirations.

She stopped the exercises and stared across the icy, barren field toward her mother's pride—the stand of white pine.

Then she turned her face away from the wind. Her legs were beginning to ache.

It was inconceivable to her that the detective from Philadelphia believed she was a murderess. Yet he did. Oh, he hadn't come flat out and said it, but his whole manner of questioning told the tale.

She could see the other elves in the kitchen now, gathering for Mrs. Tunney's breakfast. Did they know why Pratt had come? She couldn't be sure. These four retainers she had inherited from her mother always seemed to know everything. They often infuriated her in this regard. On the one hand they could be maddeningly closemouthed when she was trying to pry the truth of some situation out of them. On the other hand they were hopeless gossips blithely passing on the most ridiculous rumors.

Suddenly she realized it wasn't her elves she should be worrying about.

What about the people at Rising Moon Farm? Clifford Stuckie's sister, girlfriend, employees, and who knew how many others.

What did *they* think? What were *they* saying?

Had Pratt visited them? He had to have been there. Had he showed them a copy of the love letter? Had he hinted that Didi Nightingale was a suspect?

Of course he had. Of course.

This is the way careers are destroyed, she realized. Didi got up quickly. Her face was pale under the ski mask.

She had worked fifteen hours a day seven days a week to build up her veterinary practice over the last few years. Now it could all come tumbling down. In the popular perception, murderesses are not good vets.

She moved swiftly toward the house, trying to fight off her growing fear and panic. It was clear what she had to do. She had to go to the Rising Moon Farm. Now. Alone.

They were breakfasting in Allie Voegler's unmarked police cruiser, parked near the roadside stand on Route 44.

The menu was simple. Two whole wheat donuts and coffee for John Paul Pratt. A jelly donut and coffee for Allie.

"How was the motel?" Allie asked.

"I've been in worse," replied Pratt.

Allie studied his donut. He didn't feel like eating. He was nervous. He had to talk to Pratt but he didn't know how to go about it. The Philadelphia cop was sharp and experienced. Pratt probably cleared more homicide cases in a single month than he had in all his six years with the Hillsbrook police force.

Pratt finished off the first donut, then rolled down the window and lit a cigarette. The sudden burst of cold air almost upended their coffee containers.

"I think you're barking up the wrong tree," Allie said.

Pratt stared at the wildly swirling smoke from his cigarette.

"You should have told me you two were an item," he finally replied, censure in his voice.

"We're not an item," Allie retorted. "I wish it was so. But it isn't."

"Too bad. She's good-looking."

"And she's also one of the kindest people I've ever met. Stab someone thirty or forty times? No way. Look, Pratt, you want to know what kind of person Didi is? If this road was mined and there was a calf on the other side, bleating because its mother wasn't around, she'd walk right across the damn minefield without a second thought. I'm not even talking about a sick calf—just a lonely one. Didi Nightingale wouldn't kill a housefly."

Pratt grinned. "I should have a dime for every killer who loved his dog. I'd be a very rich man. Besides, she's a vet, isn't she? She puts animals down routinely."

"That's one thing. Murder is another. Anyway, she was home sleeping that night."

"So she says."

"There were people in the house with her. They can confirm her alibi."

"I don't consider those people credible."

"But they saw her doing her yoga exercises the next morning. She always does them right by the kitchen window."

"Means nothing. Stuckie was murdered between two and three in the morning. If it was the earlier time, she could have made it back to Hillsbrook in time to be seen at six."

"That's driving some."

"She's young. She's strong. She has a fairly new vehicle."

John Paul Pratt then ate his second donut. Allie still couldn't eat. He sipped his coffee.

"I don't trust your friend, Allie. She's too damn good to be believed."

"What do you mean?"

"You know. Too good. Hell, she's a pretty young woman with a great body and a sharp head, and she acts like a hausfrau."

"She just seems like that because she works all the time."

"Does she drink?"

"Not really."

"Pot?"

"No."

"Harder stuff—cocaine?"

"Hell, no!"

"Sleep around?"

Allie remained silent.

"Sleep with anyone?"

"Not that I know of."

"Maybe, Allie, there's a lot about her that you don't know."

Allie Voegler was beginning to feel extremely uncomfortable under the questioning. But something else was also tugging at him. A kind of enlightenment. At one level, Allie shared Pratt's cynical, disbelieving view of Didi.

Pratt lit another cigarette.

"Let me tell you a story," Pratt began. "About six months ago there was a very ugly homicide in Philly. Three teenage kids sitting on a project bench. They may or may not have been dealing drugs. Someone walks up behind them and . . . *Pop. Pop. Pop.* One round into each kid's neck, .44-caliber slugs. Two die instantly. The third is paralyzed. A week later we get a tip on a neighborhood resident. We take him in and question him. He breaks down in five minutes. Yeah, he did it. He was tired of their noise. The killer was, in everybody's opinion, a genuinely good man. He loved kids and animals and gave to the United Fund. Do you get what I'm saying?"

"Yeah, sure."

"Bad people kill. Good people kill. It's only the in-between people who don't. Like you and me, Allie. Like most people."

Allie bit into his donut. The jelly spurted out onto his collar. Disgusted, he flung the remains out the window. He wondered whether he should get out of the car and buy one of the whole wheat donuts that Pratt seemed to relish.

"Did you know who Stuckie was?" Pratt asked.

Allie shrugged. "A rich guy who played at farming."

"More than that. The Stuckies have been generous people. What's the word? Benefactors. Over the years they gave all kinds of money for all kinds of projects in the Philadelphia area—from museum wings to soup kitchens."

"So?"

"So there's a lot of pressure in this case. And I mean a lot of pressure. The kind of pressure that you can't even conceive of in a small town like this."

Allie bristled. He didn't like the urban/rural dichotomy Pratt seemed determined to erect. Any more than he liked Pratt's easy overfamiliarity—calling him Allie after he'd known him only ten minutes, patronizing him as if Allie were one of Pratt's little nephews or something.

"And there's a special reason why people are uncomfortable about it," Pratt added.

"What?"

"It had all the ugly hallmarks of a gay murder."

"Are you serious?"

"Damn serious. In fact, the minute I got to the crime scene that's what I thought. I had seen it all before. Understand? Upright heterosexual citizen goes on a bender. Picks up a hustler. Takes him to apartment. Gets robbed, sliced, and diced. Real familiar stuff. The trouble is, Stuckie was very straight. No skeletons in the closet. No closet. Everything seems to be out in the open. Except for that young lady in the big white house."

"What young lady?"

"The good Dr. Nightingale. Our angelic little vet with the foxy body. Or should we call her Madam Ice Pick?"

Allie started the car.

Didi parked her red Jeep and walked to the front gate of Rising Moon Farm.

The gate was open and in the front driveway was a large pickup truck. Didi recognized the three men standing beside it. The older man was the foreman, Herb Donizet. The two younger men were his assistants—the brothers Ike and Wilbur Flohr.

Didi stopped. She stared at the strange building at the end of the driveway. When first built, it had astonished the residents of Hillsbrook. They had never seen a structure like it.

It was a single large stone horseshoe with huge windows.

The living quarters were at the center. Radiating out both left and right were the arms, with ultramodern stalls and pens for the pigs.

As for the swine-breeding efforts that went on within the structure—they surprised no one.

In Hillsbrook, and in fact throughout the county,

there was a long tradition of eccentric gentlemen farmers and even more eccentric academics breeding pigs in an effort to get the perfect pork chop.

Everyone knew there were agricultural programs in colleges that spent millions developing new breeds like Iowa 8 or Minnesota 12—none of which ever came to market or even reproduced themselves.

Clifford Stuckie's Rising Moon Farm was squarely in that tradition. There were all kinds of breeds in the stalls.

There were common breeds like Berkshire, Hampshire, and Tamworth. And there were even Tennessee wild boars, brought to Hillsbrook from the South.

Didi was very seldom called in to consult at such an operation. For all she knew, they could have been crossing and breeding for intelligence, or size, or fat content or lack thereof, or ears that would taste better when pickled. Whatever it was, it surely wasn't the age-old effort to produce more disease-resistant hogs. That would have required specialized quarantine pens and equipment, none of which were at Rising Moon Farm. It was simply a clean healthy hog-breeding station.

Didi had never wanted to get too close to the operation. She really loved pigs. Of all the farm animals, they were, in her estimation, the most complex, the most intelligent, and the most lovable. Alas, no one bred pigs as pets. Sooner or later they all met the same fate. That was the goal of pig farming: meat.

Didi was no vegetarian. She ate meat gladly—sausage, pork chops. In fact, she loved pork. But—well, it was all so sad. A well-nigh perfect beast whose only rationale for living was to die, to be slaughtered. That disturbed her.

Herb Donizet spotted her and waved.

She walked slowly toward the three men in the bitter gray morning cold.

"How are you, Doc?" Donizet greeted her tonelessly, his face a complete blank. The young Flohr brothers merely nodded.

What was she supposed to say to them? *I just stopped by to tell you I didn't slice up your boss.*

"Is anyone at home?" she asked, addressing all three men.

"Home and up," Donizet answered. "Just walk right in." Didi sensed that he was eager to get rid of her. Usually, whenever and wherever they met, the foreman would try to make conversation with her. Mostly about pigs.

There was an awkward silence. Donizet looked away. The two Flohrs studied their ice-caked boots.

Then Herb Donizet said in a measured voice, as

if Didi were a child who had to be reassured: "Just knock and walk right in."

Oh, my, Didi thought, this is going to be every bit as difficult as I feared it would be.

She walked stiffly to the door, knocked three times, and then walked inside.

It was the first time she had been in the living quarters of the strange horseshoe-shaped edifice. She was stunned by the space and light and beautiful furniture. It was plush, so unlike the spare, high-tech aluminum pens that housed the hogs.

Liz Stuckie was seated on a leather wing chair, sipping coffee from a bowl. She looked very much like her brother—blond and slight with close-cropped hair.

Carly Mortimer was leaning against a window, peeling an orange. She was a beautiful woman with curly auburn hair.

Didi had met them both before, very briefly. But that time they were wearing work clothes or some facsimile thereof. Now they were both in bathrobes.

She heard the door behind her open and felt the wind. She turned. Herb and the Flohrs had followed her in.

All three men stood there against the wall, silent.

Oh, I see, Didi thought. I'm now considered too dangerous to be left alone with Liz and Carly. I'm a real menace. And the menfolk here are playing bodyguard for the ladies.

"Would you like some coffee?" Carly Mortimer offered graciously.

Actually, neither woman showed any sign of surprise at Didi's sudden appearance. It was as if they'd been expecting her.

"And maybe a muffin?" Liz added kindly.

"Yes," echoed Carly, "wouldn't you like something to eat?"

Didi shook her head no. She now realized the stupidity of arriving without a prepared speech—without a plan of some sort. She had expected to be, if not outright reviled, then at least looked upon with suspicion. This was the last kind of reception she would have predicted: they were treating her as a psychotic.

"I'm very sorry to have barged in like this. I just wanted to speak to all of you."

Carly Mortimer laughed suddenly. It was a very strange laugh.

And then the laughter turned into a scream of rage and Clifford Stuckie's girlfriend flung the half-peeled orange at Didi's head.

The fruit missed and smashed into the wall inches away from Herb Donizet's face.

Trembling, Didi walked quickly out of the house without another word.

* * *

Not a single number in all of Charlie Gravis's selections came up in the winning Lotto number. Disgusted, Charlie ripped the tickets up and laid them on top of the morning newspaper.

Then he leaned back on his bed in the small cubicle that functioned as his bedroom. He waited. He listened. He snoozed.

When he heard the telltale sounds from the kitchen that indicated Mrs. Tunney was having another one of her innumerable decaf coffees, he swung his legs out, grimaced from the arthritic twinges, and limped out of the room, down the hallway, and into the huge kitchen.

Mrs. Tunney was at the table, blowing over the surface of the hot liquid.

"I have good news for you," Charlie said, seating himself across from her.

"That's funny, Charlie. Because I have some news for you, too. But it isn't good. In fact, it's darn bad news."

"What?"

"Do you know who that man was?"

"What man?"

"The one Allie Voegler brought here last night."

"No."

"He was a police detective from the city of Philadelphia."

"What's so bad about that?"

"He thinks our Miss Quinn killed Clifford Stuckie."

"Stuckie's dead?"

"Dead as they come, buster. And they think missy murdered that fool of a pig farmer."

"He *was* a fool, Mrs. Tunney. All those different breeds snorting around—and for what?"

She banged her hand on the table. "What's the matter with you, man? I'm not talking about his farm! Don't you understand what I'm telling you? They think our missy Quinn stabbed that man to death."

"Calm down, Mrs. Tunney. I know what you're saying. And they're plain crazy. If Dr. Quinn's a murderer, then I'm . . . I'm . . . What are you looking at me like that for?"

"What are you doing home this time of day, Charlie Gravis? Why aren't you out on rounds with Miss Quinn?"

"She told me to stay home. She said she got business to attend."

"This is all very bad, Charlie."

He wanted to rub his hands together in glee. Things were going perfectly. In fact, it was beyond belief. The whole thing was going to be so easy.

"It's like you always say, Mrs. Tunney," he said slyly. "A young woman without a steady man is apt to get into trouble."

"This wasn't the kind of trouble I meant."

"Trouble is trouble."

She grunted her agreement.

"But, listen. Here's the news I have for *you*. I was in that new stationery store in town last night."

"Buying those fool lottery tickets again, no doubt."

"Oh, no, siree. I don't do that anymore, missus."

"Good for you, Charlie. Cash is scarce."

"So it is. Well, anyway, I'm standing there talking to old Harrah's daughter—Toby, her name is—and I look down the aisle, and who do I see there but Miss Quinn's friend Rose, and she's talking to a handsome young man."

"Well, that's not news. That girl would talk to any man in town. If she isn't careful, she's going to end up . . . loose. You know what I'm talking about."

"No, no. They was just talking, that's all. Just talking and having a good laugh over some magazine. They have nothing to do with each other—not in the way you mean. Anyway, I never seen him before. So I ask Toby. She tells me he just came to Hillsbrook. He teaches at the high school. Math and computers. Oh, he's a smart young fellow, Mrs. Tunney. With a good job. He's unattached . . . and I figure he's probably some lonely in this cold old county of ours."

"How do you know he's lonely?"

"Because he goes to that shop every night. Just to browse, Toby says."

"You're right, Charlie. That fellow's lonely."

"And he's good-looking, Mrs. Tunney. Did I mention that? Clean-cut. And young. I tell you, the moment I laid eyes on him I said this one's for our young miss."

"How does he dress?"

"Very well."

"Is he healthy?"

"Looks fit as a fiddle. And a bit . . . you know what I mean."

"No, I don't."

"I mean he's looking for a woman. It's plain."

"Can't hold that against a young fellow. I know how men are."

Mrs. Tunney sipped her coffee. Charlie could see that she was giving the idea some serious thought. Some very serious thought.

After a minute, she asked, "What's his name?"

"Ed Newman."

"Now that's a fitting name for a man. Ed Newman. I like it. It has a ring."

"It sure does."

"This is not going to be easy. Miss Quinn has her mind on other things."

"Yep," Charlie agreed. "We just have to get it up

so they meet by chance. And then it'll happen or it won't happen."

"Where?"

"I could bring her to the magazine store in the evening."

"What if she doesn't want to go? What if this Ed isn't there that evening?"

"Everything's a gamble, Mrs. Tunney."

"Yes, I guess it is, Charlie." Mrs. Tunney was turning things over in her mind, savoring the possibilities. "Oh, it would be wonderful if these two got together. He sounds like such a good young man."

"That's right. And he's a full thirty years younger than the last man you tried to fix Miss Quinn up with."

"Are you looking to pick a fight with me, Charlie?"

"No. Believe me. No."

"Good. Get on it, Charlie."

Charlie sat back and smiled. The general had spoken. Yes, he would get on it. As for the real purpose of this match—well, what the general doesn't know won't hurt her.

It was noon. Didi sat in her office in the small-animal clinic—the newest addition to her mother's house. In farm country, Didi had learned quickly, she had to maintain a small-animal clinic. The reason was simple: pet owners paid their bills promptly, while dairymen and horsemen were always months behind.

The day was still dreary, the sun hidden. The lights had not been turned on. She sat in a shroud of grayness.

Am I in the midst of a tragedy or a comedy? she asked herself.

Didi felt as if she had been up for thirty-seven hours straight. The incident with the orange had been so childish . . . so dumbfounding.

She leaned forward and laid her head on the desk. It was cold to her cheek. No matter how hard she tried, this clinic addition could never be heated properly. There were constant complaints from the people waiting to see her with their sick dogs, cats, canaries, turtles, goldfish, even snakes.

Her thoughts went to that stupid love letter. She remembered most of it. Particularly the part where he characterized his love for her as "fierce."

If it was so fierce, why hadn't the fool ever said a single word? Why hadn't there been other letters? Why had he made out the envelope with an outdated first-class stamp? Why had he used the initial D, instead of addressing it to Didi or Deirdre? Why hadn't he put the word *Personal* on the bottom of the envelope so that he could be sure that she and she alone would open the letter?

She sat back in the large leather chair that she had purchased from a used-office-furniture dealer in Kingston.

A very disturbing possibility started to crop up in her mind: What if she had merely repressed certain contacts with this man Clifford Stuckie? What if she really had met him more than twice, as she claimed. What if those meetings had not really been so brief? Or not wholly professional.

What if something horrendous had happened during one of those meetings? Something unspeakable—violent, even.

What if she had simply repressed the memory of her meeting—or meetings—with the late Clifford Stuckie?

It was a classic form of denial. She knew that. She saw it every day with owners of sick farm animals. They conveniently forget traumas the animals suffered through their own negligence.

Or they blithely denied the results of tests.

She got up and started to pace.

Why wasn't she able to remember that poor man's face clearly?

Or the way he moved. Or his speech patterns.

It was so strange.

After all, she was a trained veterinarian. She could look at a moving horse and analyze that movement . . . diagnose the smallest problems by sight alone . . . by sight and memory.

But this Clifford Stuckie . . . nothing but vagueness.

The sound of the ringing telephone jarred her. She became irrationally angry at the interruption of her train of thought and picked up the receiver violently—barking "Yes!" into the mouthpiece.

There was silence.

Then she heard a demure female voice ask: "Is this Deirdre Quinn Nightingale?"

"Yes, it is. Who is this?"

"Dr. Nightingale the veterinarian?"

"Yes, yes. Who's speaking?"

"This is Gail Bechtold."

Didi had not heard from her in years.

"Oh, Mrs. Bechtold. How nice to hear from you. I saw Hiram last evening. He just showed up out here, out of the blue. He looked fine. How are you?"

"Hiram never came back home," Gail Bechtold said quietly.

"What? He told me he was driving back immediately. I wanted him to stay over, but he wouldn't."

"He didn't come back," she repeated, the voice now frightened.

"Well," Didi said, trying to determine how best to soothe the obviously troubled woman, "he may have

51

driven a few hours and then realized he was too tired to go on. He probably just checked into a motel."

"But he still should be back by now."

"Maybe he was exhausted. Or not feeling well. Perhaps he just slept late. He'll probably be home shortly."

"I told him not to go, but he wanted to see you."

"Yes, I know. It's a rough drive in this weather," Didi said.

"He insisted on seeing you. And he was so upset over this Stuckie killing."

"Yes. That was terrible."

"What do you think I should do, Deirdre?"

"Just wait a bit, Mrs. Bechtold. He'll turn up."

"No. Something has happened. Tell me what to do."

"I suppose you can call the Pennsylvania State Police. They'll contact New York and Jersey. They could put out some kind of alert. But, really, I'm sure he just stopped over in a motel somewhere and is having himself a long sleep."

"No. He would have called me."

Didi didn't know what to say.

"Thank you, anyway," Gail Bechtold said in dejection.

"Will you call me when he comes home?"

There was a long silence. Then, at last, she said simply, "Yes."

The line went dead. Didi returned to her desk and sat down.

This business of aging was complicated, wasn't it? Was it always so sad? It seemed particularly sad in Hiram Bechtold's case. Here was a man who had been so vital and so brilliant . . . a man who loved to teach and learn and practice veterinary medicine . . . all with a passion Didi had not seen before or since.

She had not wanted to let it show when Gail Bechtold was on the phone, but Didi also had a bad feeling about Hiram's whereabouts. She wondered if he was sitting on the edge of a bed in some god-forsaken motel off the Jersey Turnpike—his memory suddenly gone, his mind a jumble of thoughts he could no longer piece together.

There was a knock at the clinic door.

"Come in," she answered.

The door opened. All Didi could see was a hand snaking in, searching for the light switch.

Then a familiar figure followed the arm in.

"Yes, Abigail?"

The young woman didn't respond at first. She just stood inside the doorway and stared at Didi.

"What did you want?" Didi asked.

It wasn't easy to determine what Abigail was

thinking at any given time. Abigail was very strange. A silent, golden-haired wood nymph with—everyone said—great musical talents. Didi had heard her singing voice once or twice; it was lovely.

Abigail was a hard worker. She tended Charlie Gravis's pigs. She groomed Didi's horse, Promise Me. She fed and cared for all the yard dogs and the barn cats.

But Abigail had to be watched. She had a penchant for getting into relationships with distinctly unsavory men. If one took her into town, a wide assortment of males would begin to hover about her, like so many honeybees.

The girl finally spoke. "Charlie told me to give you a message."

Didi nodded and waited.

But all Abigail did was fold her arms and continue to look at Didi.

Finally Didi motioned angrily with her hand, bidding Abigail to continue.

"The message is—" The girl stopped there. And then burst into helpless tears.

Didi, oddly enough, understood exactly what those tears were about.

Abigail knew. They all knew. The whole of Hillsbrook knew that Dr. Nightingale had carried on an illicit affair with a wealthy man named Clifford

Stuckie, and that she had first driven the man mad with desire and then savagely murdered him.

The tears were for Didi as well as for herself and all the other elves. What would become of them when Didi went to prison for life? And perhaps some of the tears were for the poor victim, Clifford Stuckie, even if Abigail had never even known him.

"He's in the Jeep," Abigail blurted out.

"Jeep? Who?"

"Charlie. He told me to tell you he's waiting in the Jeep . . . and it's cold."

"Thank you for the message, Abigail."

Didi stood up. It was time to do some work.

Allie Voegler was writing out a summons for the illegal burning of garbage within village limits when he got the radio call from Wynton Chung, the newest uniformed member of the Hillsbrook Police Department.

Allie finished up quickly and drove to Minnetta Lane, a road that fronts the north end of the Hillsbrook Arboretum, a world-famous botanical garden with research botanists on staff.

Chung was standing in front of a late-model Ford Taurus station wagon.

The doors were open. Two of the tires were flat. Three of the hubcaps had been stolen. The trunk and the glove compartment had been rifled. And the front seat was slashed.

"It's a Pennsylvania plate," Chung said. "I called in the number."

"Good."

"I figure someone walked away from the car and the kids got to it before he got back."

"Sounds right," Allie agreed. Hillsbrook was perpetually plagued by teenage car vandals.

"Maybe," Chung continued, "he went for help to change a flat. Maybe it was a woman driver who couldn't handle a jack. Maybe she went to look for a phone."

"Could be that."

Allie looked on both sides of the road. Forest. If one needed some help, the only smart thing to do was to go back down the road. Maybe that's what the driver had done. Maybe he'll show up in a few minutes, Allie thought. There was no way to tell how long the car had been there or when the driver had left it or when it had been vandalized.

"He could have gone that way," Chung said, pointing to an old logging path that went from roadside into forest.

"Why go there?"

"Because it looks like there's a gas station down there," Chung replied.

"No gas station around here," Allie said sharply.

"Look. Down there."

Allie looked more closely. On the logging path side of the road the woods banked down sharply and one could see the top of a Quonset-type structure.

"That's not a gas station," Allie said. "It's probably one of the aboretum's labs or greenhouses. They raise a lot of seedlings."

"The driver wouldn't know that," Chung noted.

"You stay with the car," Allied ordered.

Then he started out on the logging path, toward the building.

The slushy path was narrow, ill-defined, treacherous, and steep. It dissolved footprints in seconds. Allie moved very slowly, grasping tree limbs as he went.

He spotted the body about twenty yards down the path.

Allie circled it first before approaching.

The face was a hideous blue, gray, and black. The eyes were those of an old man.

The body was stiff as a board. The man had been dead for many hours. Frozen dead.

The left side of the head was streaked with blood. So was the rock outcropping on the path.

The missing motorist was no longer missing, it looked like. It was obvious what had happened: The old man had a flat. He saw lights from the lab and thought it was a gas station, just as Chung had speculated. He walked into the woods, not realizing how treacherous the path was because it was so dark. He tripped, fell, and smashed his head on a rock. He lost consciousness. And he froze to death.

This sort of thing happened all the time in rural locations in the course of the winter. That's why motorists are warned not to leave their vehicles when they get into trouble.

Allie bent down beside the corpse, reached inside the old man's jacket and retrieved a wallet. He flipped it open.

The first thing he saw was a photo ID clipped to one side of the wallet. He didn't see the name of the institution that had issued the card right away, but, in any case, the ID had expired; the date of issuance had been more than five years earlier.

Then he read the small print at the bottom of the card. It identified the carrier as one Hiram Bechtold, faculty member of the University of Pennsylvania School of Veterinary Medicine.

"Like the Eskimos," said a voice from above.

Allie turned. Chung was staring down intently at the corpse. His weapon was half-drawn.

"What about the Eskimos?"

Chung explained. "That's what their old folks do when they feel they've become a burden to the rest of the community—they just walk out on the ice, and they lay down and die. Freeze to death. No explanations. No regrets."

"Don't get carried away, Chung. I think this old guy was just looking for help with his flat."

"You're the man," Chung said resignedly, using street language to signify that if Allie believed that's what happened, then that's what happened.

Allie smiled. Chung's mother was black, his father, Chinese. He was born and raised in Kingston, New York, a nearby town that Hillsbrook residents considered a large, dangerous city with its own customs and language. Chung and Pratt would get along fine, he thought.

Then the smile died on Allie's face.

He turned back and stared hard at the frozen corpse. He had suddenly realized that he'd heard that name—Hiram Bechtold—before.

And he remembered who had spoken that name.

Chapter 4

"Slow down!" Didi warned Trent Tucker. "You're going twenty miles over the speed limit. You can't drive this kind of car like that on a highway with crosswinds. You'll get us both killed."

Trent Tucker slowed the Jeep and moved into the right lane. The jarring and shaking moderated.

It really wasn't a long trip from Hillsbrook to Philadelphia—as the crow flies, only four or five hours. But they weren't crows, and it was hard thruway and turnpike driving, with trucks all the way.

The moment Allie Voegler had given her the bad news about Hiram, Didi knew she had to tell Mrs. Bechtold in person. But she just didn't have the strength to make the drive there and back alone, so she had brought Trent Tucker along. He was the least productive of the elves, but he knew and loved cars. He would drive anything, anywhere.

She closed her eyes and listened to the throbbing of the engine.

It was ironic that Allie would bring her the news of her old professor's death just as she was doing what Dr. Bechtold had always cautioned her against—getting into an argument with a client.

As Hiram Bechtold used to tell his students, "Remember, the sick cow is not your client. The owner of the sick cow is your client. And if you don't get along with him . . . if he thinks you're a bungler or a mystifier or a snob . . . you won't be able to help that sick animal no matter how brilliant a diagnostician you think you have become."

Her loud argument had been with Oscar Peterson. It was about his Morgan mare, called Blue.

Blue had developed laminitis, a painful and dangerous inflammation of the hoof. It usually comes from excess carbohydrate ingestion or excess exercise.

Either way, it is now understood as a local manifestation of a more generalized metabolic problem—and must be treated as such.

Old-timers scoff at this description of the disease. And Oscar Peterson had old-time views.

When Didi diagnosed Blue with subacute laminitis, she had presented Peterson with a treatment regimen. A quite simple one: phenylbutazone as an anti-inflammatory, and, to prevent further absorption of toxic substances from the GI tract, mineral oil as a laxative.

Peterson had thanked her, paid her, and then utterly ignored her advice.

When she returned for the second visit she realized that the only thing Peterson had done for Blue was to put ice packs on the affected hooves.

So Didi had begun to shout at him, warning him that he was going to lose the mare.

And he had shouted back.

A nasty argument had ensued. In the middle of it, Allie Voegler had suddenly appeared, bringing the terrible news about Hiram Bechtold.

The Jeep lurched suddenly. Didi opened her eyes.

"What are you doing, Trent?"

"Just changing lanes, ma'am."

Didi gave him a dirty look. He had to be carefully watched on the highway because he liked to play tag with those huge refrigerator trucks.

She wondered why she treated him like a child; he was only a few years younger than she. Maybe because he reminded her of all those boys in high school she had loathed—the ones who thought the universe consisted of equal parts of beer, cars, cigarettes, and naked women in magazines.

Didi shifted uncomfortably in the front seat.

She realized she shouldn't be so hard on Trent

Tucker and others like him. By the time they had reached age twenty-one the dairy farms had for the most part vanished. There was no place for those young men anymore in Hillsbrook. Those who stayed, stayed stupid.

Didi sensed Trent Tucker giving her another of those sidelong glances. He had been doing it the entire trip. Was he frightened of her now? Had he decided that the rumors about her were true—that Didi was really a murderess?

The Jeep slowed to a crawl. Traffic was clotted. Perhaps there had been an accident. And they hadn't even reached New Brunswick yet. It was going to be a long trip.

Didi flicked the cassette deck on. Patsy Cline.

Trent Tucker asked if it would be okay to smoke. Didi said no.

She sat back and listened to the songs. But neither the words nor the music nor Patsy's strong, velvety voice was really registering.

Didi was thinking what she had been thinking ever since Allie brought her the news: Why had Hiram stayed in Hillsbrook that night, after announcing that he was going to drive straight home? Where did he stay? Why had he not stayed with her?

* * *

It was not a Lotto night but Charlie showed up at the new stationery store in the village anyway.

He bought a bag of hard candies and listened to Toby Harrah talk about the old days—when her father was alive and their farm was a going concern. She told Charlie how much she missed the sound of that damn milk truck pulling up.

Charlie kept his eyes on the aisle as he pretended to be listening with body and soul to those bittersweet memories. It was hard to sort out the browsers; there were so many this evening.

"Don't you miss it?" Toby asked him directly.

Charlie stared at her. The woman looked as if she wanted an answer. But Charlie didn't understand . . . miss what?

So he came up with a safe "More than you can imagine."

Toby smiled.

Charlie excused himself then. "Looking for something to read," he said. Then he began to amble down an aisle.

Ed Newman was leafing through a computer magazine.

Charlie got ready to pounce.

He noticed that this Ed Newman seemed older and heavier than when he had first seen him. That was good. And he looked lonelier. Even better.

Charlie stepped right in front of him, saying, "Damn! I never thought I'd see you again."

Newman looked at him uncomprehendingly.

"Just never thought I'd lay eyes on you again," Charlie reiterated.

"I think you've got the wrong man."

"No. You're Ed Newman, the teacher, aren't you?"

"Yes."

"Good. I asked around. I got your name."

"Why?" the confused Ed Newman asked.

"So you know my boss?" Charlie asked.

"Boss? No."

"Dr. Deirdre Quinn Nightingale. She's a vet."

"I don't know her. I have a cat but I've never taken her to a veterinarian. She stays pretty healthy. But I read about your boss once, in the local paper. She cured an elephant in a traveling circus . . . or something like that."

"On the money, Ed. That's her. She's a top vet and a very good-looking young woman, I'm pleased to tell you."

"You are?"

"Yes, sir. Well, we was on our rounds the other day and we saw you crossing the street near the high school. And Miss Quinn—Dr. Nightingale—says, 'Now, that's the kind of fellow I want to meet, Charlie. Him . . . right there. He seems like a man I could talk to. A man who reads and hikes and listens to music. An educated man, Charlie, a man who appreciates the fine things, not one of these country bumpkins everyone's always trying to fix me up with.' "

"She said that?" was Ed's astonished reply.

"Of course she did. But now here comes the sad part, Ed. Miss Quinn says to me, 'Charlie, you have no idea how lonely I've been since I moved back to Hillsbrook.' "

Then Charlie stepped back, a grave look on his face, and waited for the hook to set before reeling the fish in.

Newman seemed to be once again preoccupied with his issue of *Wired,* flipping compulsively through the pages.

Finally he mumbled, "I don't listen to music all that much."

Charlie said nothing.

Newman replaced the magazine on the rack.

"Do you think I should call this boss of yours?"

"No," Charlie counseled. "I think you should take your cat to the clinic and get her checked out. The Nightingale Clinic is open Tuesday and Thursday from twelve noon to four."

"I'm not really very good with women," Ed New-man protested. "The other night I—well, I asked a young woman out for a drink. She turned me down. I don't know her well. We only run into each other here in the shop, and sometimes we discuss the articles in the magazines. But she said no. So, it's like I said, I'm not good—"

"Look, we all have woman trouble," Charlie said compassionately. "But, remember! The one I'm talking about spotted *you*. She's looking for *you*."

"Do you mean she sent you here to find me?"

"I say no more," Charlie intoned mysteriously. "Just remember, Tuesday and Thursday." And he walked off.

Rose Vigdor locked her three dogs in her crumbling vehicle, shook a warning finger at each to remind them of the dire consequences of acting up, then headed for the natural food store.

Her goal was chips—glorious chips. Any and every kind. Potato chips, corn chips, avocado chips, garlic chips, beet and broccoli chips.

It had been a long, cold winter for her so far, huddled in the barn with that damn cranky wood-burning stove next to the door. She couldn't cook. All she did was drink hot tea, eat oranges, and devour bags of chips.

Actually, she had never felt better in her life. Healthy, alert, stimulated. Ideas for all kinds of new projects constantly popping into her head: beds of organic brussels sprouts grown in water; a book on the history of the chip; a home-building guide for "outlaw" women; a national organization for people who survive northern winters without electricity.

All kinds of good stuff like that.

She jammed her Tibetan wool hat down on her head. Rose had not spent a single winter without it since she purchased it four years ago in a boutique on Lexington Avenue, in Manhattan.

She started to push the shop door open.

"Are you Rose Vigdor?" she heard a voice call out behind her. She turned toward it.

A middle-aged man was standing in front of the shop window. He wore an open parka over a business suit. His hat was the old-fashioned brim variety. A blue cashmere muffler hung loose around his neck.

"I'm Detective John Paul Pratt, Philadelphia Police—Homicide."

It was too dark to read the ID he was holding open a few inches from her face.

"Well, isn't that nice?" Rose quipped.

"You're a friend of Dr. Deirdre Nightingale's?"

"Two for two. Yes, I am Rose Vigdor. Yes, Didi is my friend."

"I'd like to ask you some questions about her."

Rose laughed derisively. "Why? Did she kill somebody?"

"A Hillsbrook resident, a property owner, was

murdered in Philadelphia a few days ago. I believe your friend may have been involved."

Rose's hand went up to her mouth involuntarily. Her mother had always said that her smart-aleck ways would get her into trouble one day. But wait a minute! This guy must be crazy. What the hell was he talking about? Didi, involved in a murder?

Yes, surely the man was a nut.

"I want you to tell me about her relationship with Clifford Stuckie," the detective persisted. "Do you have personal knowledge that they were romantically involved?"

"Oh, for sure. They were one of the great pairs in history. Daphnis and Chloë. Romeo and Juliet. Cliffie and Didi."

His face clouded over. "This is a serious matter, Miss Vigdor."

"That's what you think, Mr. Jones."

"Young lady, this is no time for jokes."

"That's the one thing you may be right about. But I'll tell you what it is time for—shopping. So if you'll excuse me, I've got a date with some chips. I'll be sure to tell Didi you asked after her."

Rose turned away and walked swiftly into the store. She could hear her dogs begin to yap. The chip selections had better be made quickly, she thought. She could see that Detective Whatshisname was still out there. Poor Didi. One nutty thing after another happened to her. God, what was the story on this one? As if she didn't have enough trouble with that weird crew of elves under her roof. Now she had a stumpy cop from Philly trying to pin a murder on her. . . . *Who the hell was Clifford Stuckie!?*

Didi got lost looking for the Bechtold house in Narberth, just outside Philadelphia.

They rode around for an hour until they finally pulled up in front of a huge frame house on a narrow street.

"That's it," Didi said. She remembered the porch and the jutting second floor with the high shelves of Hiram's library visible from the street if one looked up. Hiram was the only person Didi had ever met who had a genuine library in his home—separate, inviolate, filled with books and desks and comfortable leather chairs.

Trent Tucker parked the Jeep in the sloping driveway that led to the garage underneath the house.

A rather pretty middle-aged woman in a gray fisherman's sweater answered the door.

Didi stared quizzically at her for a moment. "Who are you?"

"I'm Mrs. Reiss. A neighbor. I'm staying with Gail until her husband gets back. She's very upset."

"I'm Didi Nightingale, Mrs. Reiss. A friend of Hiram's. I must speak to Mrs. Bechtold."

The older woman guided her through the house and into the kitchen. Gail Bechtold was seated at a table, playing absentmindedly with a stack of coasters, pulling them out of their rack and putting them back.

"Gail, there's someone here to see you," Mrs. Reiss said.

Gail Bechtold looked at the visitor. "You're the Nightingale girl. We spoke over the phone. I called you."

"Yes."

"We met a few years ago, at Hiram's retirement party. You're the girl from upstate New York."

"And once or twice before that, I think," said Didi. "Listen, Mrs. Bechtold—"

She brushed aside Didi's words, suddenly standing up. She was tall and gaunt, her white hair pinned back into a bun.

"He's dead, isn't he?"

"Yes," Didi confirmed.

There was a small gasp of horror from Mrs. Reiss, and then silence.

"Did he suffer?" Gail asked.

"I don't . . . think so. I don't think he even knew what happened."

Then Didi told Hiram Bechtold's widow exactly

what had been told to her by Allie Voegler. How the body was found, under what circumstances, and the probable scenario that led to his death. She told her everything she knew except for the vandalizing of the car—the looting and the slashed seats. That seemed to be of no importance and would just cause more grief. It was pointless.

When she finished she sat down across the table from Gail. The old woman had returned to her chair, returned to shuffling the coasters, but now the tears were rolling down her face. Mrs. Reiss seemed to have lapsed into some form of catatonia.

"Where is the body?" Gail asked.

"In the morgue. I identified it."

"Are you sure it was Hiram?"

"I'm sure. Your funeral home will pick up the body, Mrs. Bechtold."

The old woman's hands began to tremble. Didi reached across the table to steady her. She shook Didi's hand off almost violently.

"He went to see you," Gail Bechtold said accusingly.

"Yes, I know. He did see me. It was wonderful to see him. I asked him to stay with me."

"He always did things for young people. He always helped young people. What a fool he was."

Didi was shocked at the comment. Hiram Bechtold a fool? No. She considered him the wisest man she'd ever met.

"I have to get back, Mrs. Bechtold."

"Do you want me to thank you for bringing me the news?" Gail asked bitterly.

"No. I don't want your thanks."

"Good. Because the only thing you'll get from me is my hate."

The blood drained from Didi's face. She felt weak and nauseous. What was going on? What had she done? Why did this old woman hate her?

"Please, Gail," Mrs. Reiss said, having now recovered from her shock. "You mustn't talk this way."

Mrs. Bechtold turned blazing eyes upon Didi. "Get out of this house."

Trent Tucker helped her negotiate the driveway. She was disturbed, profoundly disturbed. She could not believe Hiram's widow hated her. Why? How? Was it simply a case of killing the messenger? No. It wasn't that. It was something else. It had to be something that went back a long time.

They climbed into the red Jeep and started the long drive home. They might not have been received well, but they had done their job well—they had brought the news.

Driving down the Schuylkill Expressway, she told Trent Tucker to be sure to observe the speed limit. He agreed. Two minutes later she cautioned him about speeding. He complained that she should stop harassing him, that he wasn't speeding at all.

Didi suddenly realized she wanted the vehicle to go slowly, very slowly. At first she couldn't understand it, but then, as they passed the turnoff for the Thirtieth Street Penn Station in downtown Philly, she realized that she was very close to that carriage house in Rittenhouse Square where Stuckie had been murdered.

In fact, because she had spent many years in Philadelphia as a student, she knew the downtown area quite well. She knew the street the carriage house was on; she didn't even need the address. She could even visualize the facade of it.

Why not go there? Why not take a look? After all, she was suspected of having been there on the night of the murder. And maybe she had been. Maybe she got up in Hillsbrook and, in a sleep-walking trance, drove to Philadelphia, killed Clifford Stuckie, and drove back. Still in that trance. After all, weren't there cases of individuals who travel—actually drive—great distances while under the influence of drugs or hypnosis? She had once read an article about a man who claimed to have fallen fast asleep in his car on the side of the road in Wheeling, West Virginia, and then awoke the next day in Wichita Falls, in Texas.

But the moment passed. She did not give the

order to turn off the road. And soon the Jeep was out of the metropolis, in Jersey, and heading north.

"When I get home," she said to Trent Tucker, "I am going to sleep for at least twenty-four hours."

This, she did.

The morning was warm, for a change. Didi felt refreshed and raring to go. It was quarter to six. She slipped easily into the lotus position and began the preliminary breathing exercises. The earth beneath her thighs felt much more welcoming than it had a mere forty-eight hours earlier.

A shadow crossed in front of her. She thought it was one of the yard dogs at first. Then the huge frame of Allie Voegler loomed up. From her position on the ground, he looked like the Jolly Green Giant in a red flannel shirt.

"I didn't hear your car."

"Me and my car move like jungle cats."

"Do you mean cats or wolves?" she said.

"How did the old lady take it?"

"What old lady?"

"What old lady do you think? Bechtold's wife."

"How could she take it?"

"What is this, Didi? You keep answering a question with another question."

"It's what I learned to do in vet school. Better to

answer a question with a question than an answer with an answer."

In silence, Allie studied the top of her head. She was playing with him again, as always. He had half a mind to tell her what she could do with that Eastern mystic vet school wisdom. On the other hand, he couldn't stop thinking about slipping his hand under her coat and around her waist.

"I have some news for you," he said, attempting to break the flow of those thoughts.

Didi suspended her exercises, standing up nimbly but remaining in exactly the same spot.

"First of all," Allie said, "they now have an autopsy report on Stuckie. It seems he did bleed to death from the wounds, like Pratt says. What no one knew till now, however, is that he was doused with Nembutal. Not enough to kill, but enough to make him sleep like the dead. That probably explains why no one heard him scream."

"You see," Didi said wickedly, "I always sedate my victim before I slice him up. I hate to see dumb creatures suffer."

Allie ignored her sarcasm. "Pratt's gone back to Philadelphia, by the way."

"Great. Philly's loss is Hillsbrook's—"

"He'll be back, Didi. He thinks you did it. Period. He'll keep after you."

"The man's an idiot."

"I don't think so," Allie said. "Unfortunately—for you."

Didi had sensed a change in Allie's tone by then. She stared expectantly at him. But he would not meet her eyes.

"Correct me if I'm wrong, Allie Voegler," she said, "but I'm hearing something funny in your voice . . . some kind of . . . signal. Almost as if you think it's possible. As if maybe you agree with that idiot Pratt that I might have killed Stuckie."

A few seconds passed before he responded. "I don't know what I believe, Didi," he said at last. "But I know Pratt's no fool. Some of the things he says—about you—make too much sense."

"Such as what?"

"About you being so goddamn good all the time. So righteous."

"Righteous!" she snarled. "Why? Because I won't sleep with you? That makes me a self-righteous prude . . . a hypocrite . . . a killer, for god's sake? Because I won't go to bed with you?"

"I'm saying this Pratt got me to thinking about you."

Didi's voice suddenly turned arctic. "Are you here on official business, Allie?"

"Not really."

"Then get off my property."

"What are you getting so mad about?"

"Either arrest me—or whatever—or get off my property. Now, Allie."

"Didi, I'm just trying to—"

"Good-bye, Officer Voegler."

"Will you stop that!" There was a shrill, panicky quality to his voice now. "Don't you understand . . . it's that damn letter that worries me."

"What letter?"

"His love letter to you."

"You listen to me," Didi said quietly. "There's only one thing I require of a friend. It's not a difficult thing. Just the firm belief that I don't go around murdering people. You, Allie, have flunked the test. Now get out of here."

He wanted to run over to her then. Touch her, hold her, reassure her.

But Didi had turned her back and was easing into the lotus position, breathing pacifically, rhythmically, as if she were all alone on a desert island.

Allie turned and walked back to his car.

Chapter 5

Again he got the call from Wynton Chung. The young cop was almost incoherent. Allie told him to stay right where he was.

When Allie arrived at the rear of the small general store about six minutes south of Hillsbrook, Chung was grappling with a fractious young man against the hood of a car.

The young man was loud, abusive, and obviously very drunk.

Allie didn't say a word. He hit the struggling man once on the back of the head with the flat of his hand. The force slammed the drunk's face into the hood of the car, stunning him. While the man reeled, in a daze, Allie cuffed his hands behind, pulled him off the car hood, and flung him into a nearby snowbank. The man landed gently. He kept up his drunken babbling.

"You okay?" Allie turned to his colleague.

"Yeah, sure," answered the grateful Chung.

Now, for the first time, Allie could see the face of the young man sprawled in the snow. "Hell," he said in disgust, "it's Ike Flohr."

"Who's that?" Chung asked.

"One of the brothers who work at that pig farm—Rising Moon—and anywhere else they can get work."

"We have trouble with him before?"

"Used to be DWI three times a year. Then he ran over a cow in a field and they took the license away. He's not supposed to be driving at all."

"He's doing more than driving without a license."

"What do you mean?"

Chung led him to the vehicle Ike had been driving.

"Nice wheels," Allie said admiringly. And that they were. One of the long, deep pickups owned by Rising Moon.

"He was driving real erratic, so I pulled him over. Then I see this bundle of stuff on the front seat. So I ask him about it."

"What's in the bundle?"

"Jewelry. He says he's going to Albany to pawn the stuff so he can buy a balloon to fly across the Atlantic in."

"He's going the wrong way for Albany," Allie noted caustically.

He opened the door of the truck and stared at the open package on the front seat.

"I've seen this before, too," Allie said wearily.

"Do we take him in now?"

"Look, there's no point. This stuff, most of it's worthless. It gets 'stolen' by Ike every so often. He thinks it'll get him some money. The people at the farm know it's the whiskey talking. They know Ike doesn't mean anything criminal. And they know a pawnshop won't take it. So they never press charges."

"This is a helluva way to run a police department," noted a shocked Wynton Chung, still a bit frazzled from the struggle with the drunk.

"If they don't press charges you don't have a case," Allie countered. "There's no law against carrying jewelry to a pawnshop."

"Then let's take him in on the DWI."

"If you want to. Of course there's a better charge. The kid's driving with a suspended license. Like I said, I helped suspend it. But, look, Chung, half the people around here are driving without a valid license. All the damn farmers are. We leave that stuff to the state troopers. That's the way they earn their uniform allowance."

Ike Flohr was now singing in the snow.

"So I say," Allie continued, "we just sober him up and take him home."

"I don't agree with you. Drunk drivers kill—sooner or later. I say we lock his ass up and throw away the key."

"You got a point, Chung. Okay. I can't argue it. But, look. You heard what happened to the owner of that place, Rising Moon. He was murdered in Philadelphia. Those people have a lot to deal with now. Let's not give them any more grief. Next time this fool is DWI we'll throw the book at him. Okay?"

Chung shrugged. "Whatever. Like I said, you're the man. How do we sober him up?"

"Take his shoes and socks off. Put them by the truck."

"What?"

"You heard me."

"How does that get him sober?"

"It's a trick someone once showed me. For some reason drunks don't like to be barefoot, especially in the cold. So they'll do anything to get their shoes and socks on. It's hard work when you're not coordinated, but the effort gets the synapses working again. They get most of their coordination back."

"I'll try anything once," Chung said, and headed toward the snowbank. He halted midway there. "Do I uncuff him first?"

"No. Take his shoes and socks off. Bring them

near the truck. Just drop them on the ground. Then go back and uncuff him. He'll find them."

Chung walked on. Allie stared at the heap of jewelry in the bandanna on the seat. He realized he had been too quick to judge the stuff. Some of it looked real; in fact, a few pieces might have been valuable antique jewelry. There was a single-strand pearl necklace that had to be worth something.

He caught sight of something that looked like real gold. He dug out one of those old gold coins minted about 1820. This one had a beautiful design on it—a woman's figure. He had never seen such a coin, but he knew it was worth something—perhaps a lot.

Then he realized that it wasn't worth a dime, because it had been made into a key ring.

The initials on the ring part were HB.

Allie grinned. The people at Rising Moon Farm always protected the two brothers, Ike and Wilbur, when they got into trouble. But he didn't know if Ike had ever stolen any of his real boss's things—the real boss being the foreman, Herb.

Ike Flohr began to howl as Chung peeled off his socks.

Allie suddenly remembered that the foreman's last name started with a D, not a B.

The foreman's name was Herb Donizet.

Was there anyone at Rising Moon with the initials HB? He didn't think so.

Allie grimaced as he played with the coin. There was only one person with those initials who came to mind immediately—the old man who had been found dead of exposure. Didi's former professor.

Professor Bechtold. Hiram Bechtold. That was it, all right.

Now, that is strange, Allie thought.

But a good way to make some kind of contact with her again. It had been two long weeks since he'd seen or spoken to Didi.

Chung dumped the drunk's shoes and socks near the driver's seat, then went back to uncuff Ike Flohr.

Charlie Gravis was taking his afternoon nap. Someone knocked on the door. He awoke and listened. The knock came again, softly.

Charlie didn't move. It took him a long time to get going after a nap.

He didn't have to move. Mrs. Tunney poked her head in the door.

"I just heard something," she whispered conspiratorially.

"Something good, I hope."

"Not on your life."

"Uh-oh." Charlie sat up and swung his legs off the bed.

Mrs. Tunney checked behind her to make sure that no one was in the hallway. "It's about that man," she said.

"Man?"

"That young man you found . . . for Miss Quinn."

"Oh, him. What happened?"

"He came to the clinic. Today. He was the first one out there when missy opened up. He brought in a sick cat. Or at least that was the excuse he gave for showing up. He said the cat was throwing up all over the place."

"Yeah . . . and what happened?"

"Now, mind you, Charlie, I don't know for sure. I heard it from Trent Tucker, who heard it from Abigail, who was cleaning up some kind of mess in the clinic."

"What happened, for pete's sake?"

"Terrible."

"Terrible?"

"The worst. It seems that Miss Quinn examined the cat and said there was nothing at all wrong with it. And if the thing was throwing up, she said, why didn't this Ed Newman try changing its diet."

"Makes sense."

"And then this Ed . . . well . . . it seems he just flat out grabbed Miss Quinn and tried to kiss her, and missy smacked him so hard he knocked over a lamp. Well, that scared the living daylights out of the cat, who went running out of the clinic. Took close to two hours to find it. The scrawny old thing was trying to cross the highway."

Charlie didn't say a word.

"You would think Miss Quinn would be in a better mood. After all, things have calmed down with her. There's been no more talk of her being a killer, and her professor is with O'Leary in the grave. Besides, Abigail says you selected one handsome man for her. Abigail says he's almost a movie star. But she actually *hit* him, Charlie. Near knocked the stuffing out of him. Like I said—terrible!"

"That it is, Mrs. T. And sad," said Charlie.

"What a situation," Mrs. Tunney said. "I don't think that poor young man will ever speak to Miss Quinn again." She sighed heavily. "You tried, Charlie," she said with resignation and a kind of grudging affection.

Charlie waited until she was gone before he leaned back into the napping position. He grinned. Sad, eh? Well, maybe it was a tragedy for Mrs. Tunney, and maybe for Miss Quinn, too.

But what a victory for him.

Everything was going according to plan. Now it was time to implement the next step in his brilliant march toward financial security . . . and even financial excess. Excess would be no sin when the fourteen million in Lotto winnings was in his hand. Of course, he would have to compensate poor Ed Newman as well. The teacher deserved something for his hard work, didn't he?

It was getting dark. Didi stood with Abigail at the side of the house. Abigail had just laid out the dried food for the yard dogs.

Didi counted six dogs. Six of them yapping, growling, and eating ravenously from the aluminum pots that contained dried pellets, a few eggs, a few scraps of pork fat, and God knows what else.

"Where did the other two come from?" Didi demanded, half in anger, half in incredulity.

"Well, I don't know," a contrite Abigail replied.

"Look, Abigail, we can't keep adding to the flock. Do you understand what I am saying?"

"They just show up."

"And stay."

"I think they like it here."

"Are you sure our new boarders don't belong to anyone?"

"They don't have tags."

Two of the dogs were chewing at each other. Abigail calmly walked over and separated them.

The mutts had finished all the food in all the bowls in less than thirty seconds—a remarkable performance. Didi never understood why the yard dogs were always so hungry. They never did anything except occasionally chase a car or a squirrel.

Abigail and Didi headed back toward the house.

A car horn sounded, close. Then a car pulled in off the road, its lights temporarily blinding them.

The driver climbed out of the car and ambled toward them.

"It's Allie Voegler," Abigail announced, as if Didi needed someone to identify the visitor.

Allie did not greet them. Without preliminaries, he said to Didi, "Can I talk to you alone?"

Abigail turned to leave, but Didi caught her arm and forced her to stand her ground.

"Anything you have to say to me you can say in front of Abigail."

Even in the growing darkness, Allie was visibly nervous, almost bumbling. He looked very unhappy. Didi knew he had missed her these past three weeks, much more than she had missed him. But the relationship had been strained for a while, even before all this mess with the murder, what with him mooning over her incessantly. It was like Rose Vigdor said: Either sleep with the man or dump him. Why prolong the agony? It could go on for years and years.

"What do you want here, Allie?" she asked.

"I have a bit of information for you," he said stiffly.

"That's good. I need all the information I can get. Let's just hope it's information that's useful for the defense rather than the prosecution."

Didi was chagrined at her own comment. Maybe she was being too aggressive with poor Allie. Lately, she realized, she had become aggressive toward all men. Like with that fool of a man, Ed Newman, who had made a pass at her in the clinic. She shouldn't have hit him . . . not so hard, anyway. This was not the way to go. She wanted a man to love and to love her.

"We picked up Ike Flohr a short time ago for drunk driving."

"That's nothing new for him," Didi noted.

"Right. But this time he had some jewelry with him. He had taken it from Rising Moon Farm and was on his way to Albany to pawn it. For some ridiculous scheme like a balloon flight over the Atlantic. Anyway, he had a piece with him, a key chain, with the initials HB."

She started at the mention of the key chain. "Was it a gold coin?"

"Yes. How did you know?"

"An old gold coin with an engraving of Lady Liberty on it?"

"Yes."

"It is Hiram's. Was, I mean. He always carried it. He always used to twirl it when he lectured. It was like his worry beads."

"Well, I just thought you should know," Allie said, and then turned to go.

"Wait a minute." She stopped him with a hand on his shoulder, which she quickly withdrew. "Where did Ike get it? What does it mean?"

"I suppose he got it where he got all the other stuff he was going to pawn. Where he works. At Rising Moon Farm. What does it mean? I don't know."

"Where's the coin now?"

"Chung brought Ike and all the jewelry back to the farm. We're not going to press any kind of charges. And the people at Rising Moon surely won't."

One of the yard dogs began to play with Allie's shoes. He was a Rhodesian Ridgeback mix—a pretty, goofy beast.

"At least someone likes me around here," Allie said. He walked to his car and drove off.

Abigail was saying something, but Didi wasn't listening. This whole thing with the key chain was very strange. Almost frightening.

It meant that Hiram Bechtold had stopped in at Rising Moon Farm instead of going back to

Philadelphia. Then, a few hours later, he'd set out for home.

Where else could Ike Flohr have gotten the key ring? Hiram must have left it at Rising Moon. Surely if Ike had stumbled upon Hiram in the woods—dead or alive—and looted the body, he'd have taken more than a key chain.

"Abigail, do me a favor and get my parka," Didi said.

All the yard dogs were now yapping around her; they all wanted more food.

Hiram was the most honest man Didi had ever known. Hadn't he told her that he didn't know the murdered man, Clifford Stuckie? That he had spoken to him only once?

If he didn't know the Stuckies, why did he go to their farm? It wasn't to give his condolences—after all, the mourners there knew that Clifford's Rolodex had been open to the name of the Narbeth vet. They would have looked upon Hiram with as much distrust as they looked upon Didi.

Hiram had lied to her. It was as simple as that.

Whoa, Didi, she cautioned herself.

Abigail returned with the insulated parka. Didi put it on.

"Are you going out, Dr. Quinn?" Abigail asked.

"Yes."

"Do you want me to go with you?"

Didi was taken aback. It was unlike Abigail to ask such a question. Didi realized that she must look distraught, even crazy, what with all that was spinning around and around in her mind. Obviously, Abigail was worried about her.

Didi knew damn well that Allie didn't think much of the piece of information he had brought her. It was throwaway police intelligence, a way to make contact with her again. He'd come over because he loved her and missed her and the whole damn thing was going so badly.

"Just take any messages," Didi said, climbing into her red Jeep and driving off.

The tires kept spinning, seeming to moan: *Why did Hiram lie? Why did Hiram lie?* Why didn't he stop off at her place to rest? Why go to Rising Moon Farm? He must have done more than just visit. Had he slept there for a few hours? At any rate, he'd stayed long enough to misplace his key ring.

She drove to Rising Moon Farm and parked across the road from the entrance.

Several times she opened the door and got out of the Jeep, steeling herself to enter the farm's premises. But each time she stopped herself and got back in.

What was the point of going back there now?

They could simply deny that Hiram had ever been there.

They could say that Ike was one of the drunken vandals who looted Hiram's abandoned vehicle, and that was how he came to have the key chain.

Besides, Stuckie's girlfriend might attack her again . . . maybe this time with something deadlier than an orange.

She drove to the tavern on Route 44, Allie's usual hangout when he wasn't on duty. He was not there. The bar was empty. Too late for the serious early drinkers, too early for the serious nighttime ones.

Didi ordered a draft ale.

She felt alternately calm and agitated. When she closed her eyes she could see gentle Hiram in front of his class in the lecture hall, spinning that coin on a chain while he discoursed on the many warning signs of mastitis in dairy cows.

She finished her drink and walked out of the bar. She stood dumbly in the cold night air, not knowing where to go or what to do next.

A realization was taking form—something was being dredged up . . . oh . . . she could sense that . . . that she was on the cusp of some kind of intuition . . . as if she were diagnosing a sick calf with contradictory symptoms.

I want to see Rosie, she said to herself.

She got back into the Jeep and headed for Rose Vigdor's barn.

* * *

It was, as usual, a bizarre scene. A beautiful young blond woman was seated cross-legged in front of a spluttering wood-burning stove. The barn door was one-third open because there was no overhead shaft for the smoke. The wind blew in. Smoke and heat blew out. They met in a swirl at the barn door.

Rose was covered with layers of blankets over her head and shoulders.

Her three dogs were fast asleep by the stove. They didn't even move when Didi walked up.

"You're just in time for dessert," Rose announced.

"Which is?" Didi asked, sitting down next to her friend.

"Avocado chips and hot tea."

"What was the main dish?"

"Potato chips and hot tea."

Didi drank the tea. It was delicious. She helped herself to three of the tasteless chips.

"Why are your dogs so quiet?" Didi asked. She was looking particularly at Bozo, the young German shepherd she herself had brought back from a dog-breeding monastery for Rose. Bozo was a real hellion . . . but now he was in blissful repose.

"Their karmas are being rearranged," explained Rose.

Didi had another cup of tea and stared into the dying wood fire.

"You don't look well, snookums. What's bothering you?"

"A whole lot."

"Care to tell Aunt Rosie?"

"It's the pink zebra syndrome. That's what I'm suffering from."

Rose laughed. "I hope it's not a social disease."

"Worse. It's when you see a pink zebra grazing in your backyard. Now, we all know there ain't no such thing as a pink zebra. So you say to yourself that you didn't see any zebra at all, although the damn thing is still there eating up your grass."

"Some people would call that denial."

Didi suddenly leaped to her feet. She felt as if she were going to explode. The suddenness of her movement got the three dogs up and moving. Huck the Corgi growled at her.

"But it's not a pink zebra I see, Rosie. Let me tell you what I see. Hiram Bechtold being murdered. That's the first thing I see. And the second thing is that he knew the man I supposedly murdered, Clifford Stuckie, a lot better than he admitted to. And the last thing I see is that there is no way on earth that the old man drove all the way to Hillsbrook just to tell me I'm a suspect in Stuckie's murder. He came for something else . . . and he died for it."

All Rose could say was, "Wow."

"Do you have any brandy, Rose?"

"A little," affirmed Rose, who got up and went to a secret cache under the scaffolding. She returned with a bottle and poured some into each of their cups.

"What are we toasting?" Rose asked.

"You and me."

"Our friendship?"

"No, our collaboration."

"So you're finally going to help me with the barn?"

"No. You're going to help me find out who murdered Hiram and why. If we also find out who sliced that rich pig farmer to pieces, so much the better."

"Wouldn't Allie Voegler be a better collaborator for you?"

"Allie and I are no longer on speaking terms."

"Oh."

They clinked cups. Didi shivered as the brandy went down.

"I await your instructions," said Rose, pouring out a bit more.

Chapter 6

Didi sat primly and grimly in the antechamber of Dr. Louis Treat's office. Everything about the place so far seemed to reek of success. She didn't know why that bothered her, but it did. It was in severe contradiction to her own ambition, and she knew it. She loathed successful veterinary establishments and their proprietors; but that, basically, was what she was striving for: to be one of them.

Treat's office, just over the state line in Connecticut, did more than reek—it screamed. There were photos of Dr. Treat with champion racehorses and prize bulls. Photos of the good doctor with calves and various adorable litters gamboling over him. There were family snapshots . . . on sailing boats and in fancy cars and in fancy climbing gear at the side of some daunting-looking mountain.

And there were posed photos of Dr. Treat with

several men and women who must have been famous people. But Didi didn't know them.

A voice boomed out: "Dr. Nightingale!"

"Call me Didi," she said, shaking the proffered hand as Dr. Louis Treat led her into his paneled office. More photos in polished wood frames. He was wearing a sweatshirt and thick corduroy pants. He looked about fifty but he still had all his hair and it was black and long. His face reminded Didi of a bloodhound trying to smile.

"It is very good to have a colleague visit," he said, seating himself behind his desk. Didi slipped into the beautiful leather chair reserved for visitors.

He said to her immediately, "You said on the phone that you want me to tell you something about Rising Moon Farm. I'll tell you whatever you want. I just want you to know that I have a policy . . . I've always had a policy . . . to not hold back anything from colleagues. You get my drift?"

"Yes. That's kind of you."

"Shoot."

Didi laughed. She didn't really know where to begin. "Does the name Hiram Bechtold ring a bell?"

"No. A colleague?"

"Not practicing. Anyway, he's dead now."

"They tend not to practice. The dead, I mean." And Treat laughed hugely at his own joke.

Then he added, "You do know that the owner of Rising Moon is also dead?"

"Yes," Didi replied. She did not tell Treat that she was a suspect.

"Well, Didi Nightingale, I hope you're not having any trouble with Rising Moon. I found them to be the most splendid of clients. I hope you're not having any billing problems with them."

"Oh, no. Nothing like that. The few times they called on me, they paid promptly."

"Good."

Didi wondered how much she could tell this man, and how much was appropriate to tell. If she told him she was investigating the death of a friend that was tied to the death of the owner of Rising Moon, he would think she was a bit peculiar, to say the least. She had no evidence to show anyone. She had only a series of strange connections.

"Did you know Clifford Stuckie well?" she asked.

"No. Not that well. But I had a few conversations with him. We had lunch together twice."

Didi noticed something in his voice, a kind of reluctance. She didn't blame him. She had to give him a reason for being there, some explanation for why she was pumping him this way.

"You see," she said, leaning forward and lowering her voice, "I have this friend. She was having a very passionate affair with the man. Then he was murdered. It was bad enough losing him, but then she found out that he was engaged to be married to a woman named Carly Mortimer. And she just cracked up. So you see, I just want to give her the facts about this man . . . about his farm. I want to help her get over this and she needs information. I think antibiotics are good for cows, but I think reason is the best treatment for humans. Do you understand what I am saying, Dr. Treat?"

"Call me Lou. And yes, I do understand—sort of."

Didi leaned back. What a ridiculous, outsized, incoherent, lying scenario she had constructed. It made no sense whatsoever.

"What did you used to talk about during lunch?" she asked boldly.

"A whole raft of things. I really liked the man, Didi."

"Why?"

"He was a kind of stock character you just don't run across anymore. Like he'd stepped out of an old book."

"But he was a young man."

"Yes, of course. You don't understand what I'm saying. He was the kind of man who is a hell-raiser in his youth—I mean his early twenties—and then grows out of it and wants to save the world."

"I never heard he was a hell-raiser."

"That's a calm word for what he was, I think. He was a bad one . . . boozer . . . gambler . . . and he whored without stop. Pardon the use of the word. Of course, maybe if I had the kind of money he had, I would have done the same."

"What did you mean by 'save the world'?"

"You know. He turned into one of those men who think breeding the perfect pig or bull will change for the better how humans live. It was a very nineteenth-century thing."

"Then he was a serious pig breeder?"

"Oh, most definitely. I mean, I remember one conversation we had that went on for hours. About M. E."

"What?"

"You know . . . metabolizable energy."

"Yes, I'm sorry."

"Well . . . he used to print out these computer charts showing daily nutrient intakes and requirements for intermediate-weight breeding pigs. He would talk about amino acid requirements and mineral and vitamin supplementation until you wanted to crawl under the table."

"Did he ask your advice?"

"Not really. Once . . . Actually, now that you bring it up, I probably met him more than I originally said. Maybe five or six times. I remember once we had an argument about feeding. I recommended a basic corn/soybean mix in pellet form. And a small barley and cow's milk supplement. At the time he was big into sorghum. With specific vitamin supplementation. And he had a kind of weird passion for peanut meal."

Dr. Treat stopped talking and stared at the ceiling. He might have been following the movement of a fly on the ceiling. But it was the dead of winter. There were no flies.

He looked at her. "You know, I'm glad you're asking me these questions."

"Why?"

"Because it makes me think about Rising Moon Farm. In fact, now that you've brought it up, I must say it was a very peculiar place."

Didi leaned forward. Her heart was beginning to pump a bit. She was on the chase now. She could feel it.

"Oh, not the farm itself. I mean my relationship to it."

"Were you on retainer?"

"Yes. And a healthy retainer it was. More like a racetrack contract, and I treated it as such. Except instead of visiting the horse stalls every morning, I peeked into the pigpens twice a week."

"What was peculiar, then?"

"That nothing ever happened. No pigs were ever sick. They ran a spotlessly clean operation. But come to think of it—for a breeding farm there were damn few litters."

He laughed nervously. "Of course, they were always shipping pigs in and shipping pigs out. And that foreman—what's his name . . . ?

"Herb Donizet."

"That's right. Well, he used to wave slips of paper in front of me with Stuckie's latest explorations in genetic theory and practice. Which kinds of pigs to be crossed. Stuff like that. But I never even looked at them."

"Did you know the women at the farm?"

"Once or twice they invited me for coffee when I was there in the morning. I like them both. The sister and the fiancée. They're quite knowledgeable about swine."

"Yes, they seem to be," Didi said, as if she too had some kind of professional familiarity with them.

"I suppose," he said, "when your family has that kind of money you really don't have to make a living out of breeding. So you can theorize a lot . . . and just play around. Of course, I never saw his beef-cattle-breeding operation down in Florida. Maybe it's different down there."

"Did you ever have dealings with those two brothers? You know, the hands at the farm."

"Not really. They used to handle the menial stuff when I came by. Why?"

"Just curious."

He stared at Didi. "Did this friend of yours really love Stuckie?"

"I'm afraid she did," Didi replied, trying to look bereft.

"He was a handsome man."

"Yes, he was."

"Is your friend a vet also?"

"Oh, no. She just lives close to me in Hillsbrook."

"He didn't strike me as the kind of man who would cheat on a fiancée."

"But you said he whored a lot when he was younger."

"That was then. This is now. I told you, the man had changed profoundly."

"Yes, you told me."

"Is there anything else?"

"Not really."

"Then you tell me about *your* practice," Louis Treat demanded, laughing.

"What is there to tell?" Didi retorted in a kind of deprecatory tone.

But then she started talking.

Charlie knocked three times very quickly. There was no answer. He knew this was where Ed Newman lived. There was only one Ed Newman in the village, and he lived on top of the supermarket on Main Street.

Charlie stared down the short alley. Maybe the entrance was on the main street and not on the side. But it was this door that held the scribbled names, three of them, one being Newman.

It was a dreary day, wet and cold. Charlie was wearing his snow jacket and an old felt hat that used to have a feather in it. He kept blowing on his hands and stomping.

He knocked five times more and when no one answered he threw caution and dignity to the wind.

Stepping back, he shouted, "Ed! Ed Newman!"

A window on the second floor opened and a face peered first out, then down.

Charlie couldn't see the face of the man who called down, "Who's there?"

"It's Charlie Gravis. Looking for Ed Newman."

There was no answer. Charlie strained his eyes. It sure seemed like Ed Newman—the shape of the head was the same.

Then the window slammed shut. Charlie edged back to the door. He listened. Yes . . . those were footsteps.

The door swung open and there was Ed Newman, looking underfed and defiant.

"What do you want?" Newman asked angrily.

"I just want to talk to you a bit."

"You don't have a damn thing to tell me. You're the one who got me in all this trouble. You're the one who made me act like a fool."

"I don't know what you're talking about, Ed, if you don't mind me calling you Ed."

"You must know what happened in the clinic by now. You know what I did," he said, his voice cracking with shame.

"That's nothing to really worry about."

"Nothing to worry about! Are you crazy? I lost control of myself. I all but attacked a woman, a complete stranger. I tried to kiss her, for god's sake. But I wouldn't have if you hadn't lied to me, old man. You told me she fell for me, just after seeing me cross the street. You set me up!"

"Ed," said Charlie, putting his hand on the younger man's arm in a grandfatherly gesture, "I think you ought to let me speak to you for a few minutes. Just give me a few minutes."

Ed Newman glared at him, then shrugged and motioned for Charlie to come in.

Charlie climbed the steep, narrow stairway very slowly. Those old bones were creaking, but Charlie was smiling in spite of them. Because he knew young Ed Newman was now perfectly ripe to be plucked.

Once inside, Charlie felt even better; what an unrelentingly gloomy place it was. A small bed. A low table with a TV set. Two chairs, one of which was occupied by a glowering cat. A tiny walk-through kitchen. Who wouldn't want to make enough bucks to leave a place like this far behind him? This place was little better than a cell.

"Talk fast; I'm not really anxious to hear anything you have to say."

Charlie sat down in the empty chair and waved to the cat.

"It will all pass over," the old man said pleasantly.

"Pass over? Don't you understand what happened in the clinic? I grabbed her and tried to kiss her and she had to fight me off. Do you understand how crazy I acted? I can't believe now that it was me! I mean, suppose she had called the school to complain. Suppose she had involved the police. I can't even bear to think about it."

"People act strange in clinics," Charlie noted. "Even the animals act strange. One time, I remember, someone brought in a dog who just had a cut paw. The dog lays down and just dies. Right there. It died. And no one knew anything until the dog's turn came to be examined."

Ed Newman made an ugly sound, went to the refrigerator, took out a bottle of beer, and sat down on the bed, shaking his head.

Charlie Gravis purred. Yep, the young man was taking to drink.

"I couldn't help myself," Newman said in a dramatic whisper.

"Can't hear you."

Ed Newman got off the bed and walked very close to Charlie. "Now can you hear me? I couldn't help myself. The minute I walked into that clinic and saw your Dr. Nightingale I fell in love. She took my breath away. She's beautiful and smart and you could see the kindness and gentleness written all over her. Do you understand? This was the woman I had been waiting my whole life for. This was the real thing. At first I was so overcome I couldn't even give her a good fake story about my cat."

He looked at the beer as if it were loathsome and he slammed the bottle down on the TV table.

"Now can I say a few words?" Charlie said gently.

"Sure. Say what you have to say and then get out of here."

"Please sit down."

Ed Newman again took his seat on the bed. The cat jumped off the chair and joined him.

Charlie waited a few minutes before saying mildly, "There's something you have to know, Ed."

"I'm waiting."

"That passion and love you say you felt when you saw her . . . well, she felt the same way."

Ed Newman was struck dumb.

"Do you hear me, Ed?"

"What are you saying!"

"I heard that she felt the same thing but she had to slap you because she was afraid of getting involved."

"What is there to be afraid of?"

"You're a schoolteacher."

"And proud of it."

"But you're going to die poor. And Miss Quinn has taken a kind of vow to marry only a man with money. It's not that she's greedy or anything. It's just that she has a lot of mouths to feed, you know. And she had to fight very hard to save her mother's land and house and to build a practice. So you see, she couldn't let herself go no matter what she felt for you."

"I don't believe you."

"I live in her house, Ed. I work side by side with her. I know of what I speak."

Newman threw his head back in disbelief and perplexity.

Charlie waited a long time. He could hear the steam hissing out of the small primitive radiator by the window.

"All you need is twenty million dollars," Charlie finally said, calmly.

Ed laughed uproariously.

"I'm an old man, Ed. I'd like to see Dr. Quinn taken care of before I die. I want her to have a man she loves. A man with money and property and respect. And I want her to have a big family. I like you, Ed. I respect you. I know you want the same things for her that I do."

Charlie paused and shifted in his chair. His right foot had fallen asleep.

"Ed, what if I told you I could get you at least seven million dollars . . . in cash . . . within the next fourteen days?"

"What is this? Some kind of Faust thing?"

"I don't know anybody named Faust."

"It's a story. About a man who sells his soul to the devil."

"I ain't no devil, Ed. And it's not your soul I'm interested in. Believe me."

Ed Newman rose, retrieved his beer, and took a long swallow from it. Then he poured the rest of the bottle out into the sink. He washed out the bottle slowly and fastidiously.

"Are you serious?" Ed finally asked.

"Do I look like I'm fooling?"

"Well . . . no."

"In fact, the last time I was this serious was on Iwo Jima, and that was more than fifty years ago."

"Are you talking about something criminal?"

"No, sir."

"Sunken treasure?"

"No."

"What, then?"

"The lottery."

"You mean the New York State Lottery? You mean Lotto? That ridiculous game for fools who like to write numbers down on tickets?"

"The prize is now almost twenty million."

"And you and I are going to win it?"

"And split it—sixty-forty."

"You're even nuttier than I thought." He laughed. "How?"

"Because you know computers and you know math."

"A lot of people know computers and math. I don't hear about them winning millions."

"Because they don't have me. I know what to look for."

"What?"

"It's simple. You just program the computer so it reads every winning number since the beginning of Lotto. And then your computer finds out which numbers have been underrepresented. And these are the numbers to play. It's called, I think, the law of probability. And then you get those math formulas working and you figure out how to combine all those underrepresented numbers along with some hot numbers . . . and boom."

"What does 'boom' mean?"

"All those millions come rolling in and everybody's happy."

"You've been thinking about this, haven't you?"

"A long time."

"I don't know what to say."

"What is there to say? You have nothing to lose."

"There are things like self-respect," Newman said.

"I lost that when I lost my farm."

"That's a sad thing to say, Charlie."

"Well, you finally called me Charlie."

"Did you tell me the truth?"

"About what?"

"About Dr. Nightingale?"

"As close to the truth as an udder is to the milk."

"Tell me what to do."

They were seated in a booth in the Hillsbrook Diner, facing each other.

Didi's rare cheddar cheeseburger had just been served.

Rose's Greek salad was already on the table.

"What did you learn from the vet?"

"Dr. Louis Treat told me nothing in the guise of telling me a lot."

"Which means?"

"Well, he said whatshisname, Clifford Stuckie, was a very bad boy when he was young . . . drinking and gambling and, what was the word he used, whoring."

"All young men do that. That's not being bad anymore."

"I guess not. Anyway, Clifford Stuckie, it seems, grew out of it and began to fancy himself a world-class breeder of pigs and bulls. So says Dr. Treat. The problem is, as Treat puts it, Rising Moon doesn't really seem to be a serious swine-breeding station. At least not by Treat's standards. But they run a good operation, he notes. Of course, Dr. Treat has a yearly contract with Rising Moon Farm, so you have to take everything he says with a grain of salt."

"I forget why we are concentrating on Rising Moon Farm, Didi."

"Because that's where Hiram stayed before he was murdered."

"If he was murdered."

"Oh, he was murdered, all right. And that's where Stuckie and his family and friends stayed. And the connection between Stuckie and Hiram had to at least start at Rising Moon, no matter where it ended up—in Philadelphia or Timbuktu."

"And that's where Stuckie lost his heart to you, Didi, and started to grieve and began to write you love poems and love notes. I remember one well, Didi. It starts out: 'To my Beloved Veterinarian . . . the pigpen's a fine and quiet place, but none I think do there embrace.' "

"That isn't funny, Rose."

"Sorry."

Didi, using her knife and fork, ate a quarter of her cheeseburger. Rose picked at her salad, having questioned earlier the freshness of the lettuce.

"Let's get down to business," Didi said, pushing the bulk of the burger away.

"Did you bring the list?"

"Yes," Didi replied. "Did you bring the chart?"

"Of course," Rose said. She reached down beside the booth and pulled up a huge, impressive-looking chart with all kinds of different color markings on it.

Didi smiled as she perused it. Rose had followed instructions brilliantly. It was an economic chart, purportedly measuring the dollars family farms pump into the New York State economy through the purchase of goods and services like feed, grain, household and farm implements, and so on.

"Perfect, perfect," Didi said, then, looking up, added: "Let's hear the cover story."

"First the list," Rose said stubbornly.

Didi pulled out a crumpled piece of paper and placed it on the table.

"You have to make only three stops because there

are only three real feed and grain dealers left in all of Duchess County. All within a fifty-mile radius."

Rose looked at the list, then pulled out a map of Dutchess County and consulted it earnestly. Then she affixed the piece of paper to the map with a paper clip, folded the map, and put it into her knapsack.

"I still don't get the point of all this," she admitted.

"We have to find out what kind of operation Rising Moon Farm really is. You are what you eat, Rose. You above all believe that. And you are what you buy." Didi laughed a bit nervously. "Besides, I can't think of anything else to do right now. I'm confused. Now, your cover."

Rose sat back.

"Okay. My name is Rose Vigdor. I live in Hillsbrook but I am a graduate student in agricultural economics at the State University of New York at Cobleskill. My graduate thesis is the relationship of farm subsidies in New York State to farm expenditures. My study is restricted to three types of family farms: livestock, dairy, and produce. But within each of these categories are included both business and domestic expenditures."

"Excellent. Excellent. It's very believable."

"Thank you. Then I tell them that the study is blind—we're not interested in the names of the proprietors or the names of their operations. This is to insure anonymity. All we want are blind computer printouts of each of the dealer's farm customers in these categories. It is a very important study and it has been funded in part by grants from the United States Department of Agriculture and the New York State Council for Business Development."

"Beautiful! It sounds very official. If I were a feed and grain dealer, I wouldn't dare not give you the information."

"I am weaving a web of deceit here, madam," Rose said.

"Aren't we all? By the way, Rose, if they tell you they can't provide you with the information because all their customers in the categories you mentioned pay cash, they're lying. So just keep after them. No farmer pays on time and no farmer pays cash. To survive, they need credit lines at the local bank and bills are paid and monitored off those accounts."

"And you want all purchases?"

"Yes. But remember, feed and grain dealers don't sell a big variety of products."

"I'm going to do my best, Didi. I think the only thing that will hamper me is the fact that I don't have my New York clothes. I dumped all of those things in thrift stores when I moved up here. It would have been nice if I could dazzle them."

"Relax, Rose. I don't think dazzle is called for."

Didi ordered a cup of coffee. Rose ordered hot water with a wedge of lemon; she had brought her own herbal tea bag.

Didi sipped the coffee and grimaced.

"Bad?" Rose inquired.

"No, it's not the coffee. For some reason I just thought of Gail Bechtold's obvious hatred of me when I brought the bad news. It was so strange. And her seeming hatred for all young people. As if they were responsible for Hiram's death."

"Well, if it was a murder, maybe young people did it."

"But she doesn't know yet that her husband was murdered."

Rose gave a knowing chuckle. "So you think."

"Wait. What are you saying? Do you know something I don't know and should know?"

"Calm down, calm down," Rose said, holding up her hands in mock self-defense. "I was just talking through my hat."

"Sorry I jumped on you. It seems I jump all the time now." She leaned forward and motioned that Rose should do the same. "You know," she continued, "I can't go anyplace public anymore without thinking someone is watching me . . . without thinking that someone is saying, 'There goes Didi the vet . . . the little tramp who stuck a knife into that man.' "

"I assure you," Rose said, "no one in this diner is looking at you."

"Good."

"Any last instructions?"

"Yes. Don't force the issue."

"Understood."

"And something else. Be careful."

"I am always careful, girlfriend."

That struck Didi as very funny. Anyway, she knew it wasn't true.

It had once been a nice motel. Now it was a classically seedy one, with a motel clerk to match, John Paul Pratt thought as he stood in the tiny lobby. There was a bulletproof partition over the cashier's window. It looked like a check-cashing office in downtown Philly, even though the locale was suburban Cherry Hill.

Pratt studied the clerk from a distance. He never questioned a person without evaluating him first. This clerk, Pratt knew, lived on tips. It had to be, what with three-hour and even one-hour rental of rooms.

Like the motel itself, the clerk looked as if he had seen better times. He was not a young man. His suit jacket was rumpled and he wore no tie. His bulbous stomach hung over his pants and his face was florid. Alkie, Pratt thought—a classic alcoholic.

To get the most mileage out of this clerk he would have to be gentle. Not hard. But it all depended on whether the clerk made him as a cop quickly. If he did, there was no point in being subtle.

Pratt was weary. He had spent the better part of the last three days going from motel to motel between Hillsbrook and Philadelphia along a fifteen-mile-wide corridor.

He carried with him a recent photo of Clifford Stuckie that he had obtained from Stuckie's fiancée. And a blown-up glossy of a newspaper photo showing Deirdre Quinn Nightingale next to a circus elephant she had cured of some disease.

How many motels had he been in so far? Twenty-five? There had been no firm identification yet, but he had a very strong hunch that he would hit pay dirt soon. The affair between Stuckie and Nightingale had to have been clandestine to the nth degree; that was why no one in Hillsbrook knew about it. He guessed that they had rendezvoused at motels along the route between Hillsbrook and Philadelphia.

The clerk spotted him, stared for a moment, and then ignored him.

Pratt decided this was no time or place for subtlety.

He walked to the desk and flashed his ID. The clerk didn't even look at it.

Pratt laid out the two photos side by side on top of the desk, about ten inches away from the man's protruding stomach.

"Have you seen either of these people within the last six months?"

The clerk didn't look at the photographs.

"I don't look at people's faces," he said.

"Why is that?"

"I scare easy."

"You make my life hard," Pratt said in a low, angry voice, "and I'll lay some fear on you the likes of which you have never known."

"A nasty cop. How unusual."

"You have no idea," Pratt retorted.

The clerk heaved a sigh, dug into the pocket inside his jacket, and came up with an antique glasses case. Slowly, very slowly, he opened the case and removed the eyeglasses. Then he pulled out his handkerchief and cleaned the lenses.

He slipped the glasses on and leaned over the photos, not touching them at all.

"What did they do?" the fat man asked.

"Robbed a big motel near Devon. Murdered the clerk." A good lie, Pratt thought. There's no interest like self-interest.

The clerk picked up Stuckie's photo and stared at

it more closely. He shook his head. "I mean, no and yes. I see a hundred guys a week who could look something like this. But do I remember this one in particular? No."

He put the first photo down and picked up the other one. He looked at it. He removed his glasses, rubbed his eyes, and put the spectacles back on. He tilted the photograph this way and that, closer to his face, then further away; closer to the lamp, then in shadow.

"How long ago did you say?"

"It could be any time during the past six months."

"Well, I'll tell you . . . about eight weeks ago a broad came in here. She rented a room. About an hour later a guy shows up. They rented the room for twenty-four hours but I only saw them once."

"Is that the one?" Pratt asked anxiously, tapping Didi's photo with his finger.

"It might be her. She had that kind of face—kind of . . . saucy. Yeah. What do they call it? Pert. And she was built like that. But it was the clothes I remember the most and they're way different."

"What kind of clothes?"

"A definite knockout. She came in with a long coat, one of those range-rider things. When she took it off she was wearing a dress that seemed to be made of rope. The ropes were wide apart. You could see through them easy. And underneath she was wearing a red bra and red panties. It was wild."

"You think this was her?"

"Maybe."

"Did she use her credit card?"

"No. I remember she paid cash. Two fifty-dollar bills."

"Did she sign the register?"

"I don't know. I guess so. But it was probably a phony name, and since I don't remember it, what's the point of looking?"

"Just look."

"In a few hours. When I get off."

"No, friend. Look now."

The fat clerk clucked his tongue in disgust and pulled out two ledgers from beneath the counter.

He flipped the pages, located the section he was seeking, and went down the names methodically, using his finger as a guide.

He found nothing to jog his memory.

"Keep looking," Pratt ordered, and then he went to the pay phone.

Allie was lying fully clothed on the unmade bed in his apartment when the phone rang.

He let it ring. The machine kicked in. It was Pratt. He left a New Jersey number and told Allie to call him back the moment he got in, no matter what time it was; Pratt would be waiting.

Let him wait, Allie thought. He felt miserable. He had started drinking too early in the day and had ended up drinking too much. In addition, the pot roast he had eaten in a roadside diner had made him sick. Pot roast always did him in, but he kept ordering it. The gravy was the prize.

He covered his eyes with his arms. The thing with Didi was getting him down. Nothing like this had ever happened between them. Oh, they had had fights because she wouldn't sleep with him or marry him or go out drinking with him. Stuff like that. But this time she had said she really didn't want to see him anymore. She had accused him of being an unfaithful friend.

He squirmed on the bed. She had been so right. Pratt's suspicions had registered with him—at the time. Now he really didn't know. And the bizarre thing was that, even though he was a police officer, he really didn't care. More to the point, he'd never really believed that she killed Clifford Stuckie. But the possibility of an affair and the power of the love note were evident to him. And, yes, damn it, he was jealous. It was all a jumble. An awful jumble of misunderstandings that had just gotten out of hand.

He sat up and looked around wildly, his stomach

churning. He walked around the apartment a few times, holding his hands high to ease the nausea.

Then the stomach pain subsided.

I ought to call Pratt, he thought. The arrogant bastard.

He dialed the number. Pratt picked up on the first ring. "Allie?"

"Yeah. Just got in."

"I'm in a motel in Cherry Hill."

"Where's that?"

"Jersey. Just outside Philly. I got a clerk here who made a tentative ID of Nightingale."

Allie felt a shiver.

"What kind of ID?"

"Off that circus photo. A woman close to that description checked into this motel about eight weeks ago. A guy joined her a few hours later . . . could have been Stuckie."

"How sure is he?"

"Not sure enough. But he remembered her clothes when she checked in."

Allie sat down on the edge of the bed, afraid. It was freezing in his apartment but his forehead was now beaded with sweat.

"Allie, are you there?"

"I'm here."

"I need some help."

"Sure, John."

"According to the clerk, she came in with one of those range-rider winter coats. Have you ever seen Nightingale wear one of those in Hillsbrook?"

"I don't know what you mean by range-rider coat."

"They're long and usually made of canvas, with a high collar. Drug dealers wear them a lot, but in leather."

"We don't have any drug dealers in Hillsbrook in black leather coats."

"It doesn't have to be black. Look, they're in Western movies . . . the outlaws usually wear them. Clint Eastwood always wore them in those spaghetti Westerns."

"I think I know what you're talking about."

"Well, does she have one?"

"I never saw her wear one. In the winter she usually wears a parka."

"Okay. Let's leave that alone for now. There's more. The clerk said underneath she was wearing a very hot number. A kind of see-through rope dress—and what you saw was a red bra and panties."

There was silence.

"Allie?"

"Yeah. What are you asking me?"

"Did you ever know her to wear such an outfit?"

"Don't be stupid. No."

"Are you sure?"

"I'm sure."

"Well, ask around. I'll be in touch. Remember, that darling Clementine of yours probably had at least three lives you didn't know about. And in two of them that kind of outfit was on the menu. Take care."

Allie stared at the phone for a long time, and then, in a rage, he yanked mightily at the receiver, ripping the wires from the wall. He picked up the whole apparatus and flung it across the room. He saw the plastic casing of the phone shatter.

"What am I doing?" he said aloud, to no one. He sat back down on the bed.

His friendship with Pratt had just ended, he realized. Along with all professional courtesies.

It didn't matter whether Didi was guilty or innocent of anything. It didn't matter whether he was a police officer or not.

One thing was sure from now on. He would not participate in the crucifixion of the woman he loved.

Pratt looked up from the frozen street. He could see a light on the second floor of the carriage house. Good, the caretakers were in.

He slammed the antique brass knocker several times as hard as he could. It was lost in the night traffic sounds of downtown Philadelphia. In Hillsbrook, he realized, the sound would have traveled a long way . . . a long way indeed.

Then he saw the bottom of the carriage house light up and the door swung open.

It was Junior Walls, in pajamas, an army surplus field jacket thrown over them.

"Who are you?" the young man asked.

Pratt could see the wife, Pilar, behind him. She was wearing a long sweater over her nightgown.

"Who's out there?" Junior demanded again.

The detective didn't answer.

"Oh, it's you," said Walls with disgust and hostility. "Why don't you leave us alone? We told you everything we know. When will this end?"

Pratt pushed past him into the small house. The first thing he saw was the restored carriage. It dominated the ground floor.

"This won't take long," Pratt said. "In fact, you might find it enjoyable. It's picture time."

He climbed up onto the carriage and laid the two photos out beside him. Then he patted the seat opposite. "Come, children, join your uncle John for a little sleigh ride in the snow."

Grumbling, the two young caretakers climbed up onto the carriage and sat down.

"Now, this one you know, don't you?" Pratt asked, holding up the photograph of Clifford Stuckie.

"Yeah, we know him," Junior said.

"Knew him," Pilar corrected.

"Do you think the Stuckie family will kick us out? Close this place up?" Junior asked.

"I don't know. They didn't say," Pratt replied. He picked up the other photo, the glossy one, blew on it, and handed it to Junior. "I want you to look at this photo very carefully," he cautioned.

Junior held it gingerly and stared. Pilar stared over his shoulder. Pratt studied the two as they studied the photo. They were a handsome young black couple. Typical Philly students. Junior was the darker of the two. He was well-built, like a gymnast. Pilar was a bit taller than he, and willowy. Pratt had checked them out. They were very good in their fields. Pratt wondered how the hell they were ever going to earn a living at jazz and ethnomusicology. They should take some accounting courses.

"Who am I supposed to be looking at . . . the elephant or the lady?" Junior quipped.

"Don't get smart with me, sonny. Do you know her?"

"No."

"I don't either," Pilar volunteered.

"Have you ever seen her . . . anywhere?"

They shook their heads.

"Who is she?" Pilar asked.

"Her name is Deirdre Quinn Nightingale. She's a veterinarian. She's the woman Stuckie wrote the love letter to."

"I thought Stuckie liked buxom women," Junior said.

"Why do you say that?"

"Well, I did meet whatshername—his fiancée. She's a big woman."

"Statuesque, fool, not buxom," Pilar said, almost giggling.

"What other women did he bring here?"

"Here?" Junior asked, surprised.

"You heard me."

"None."

"You're lying."

"Well," Pilar jumped in, "he's only half lying, and that's because he doesn't know. We thought he brought others but we couldn't be sure. Sometimes we heard him come in and he wasn't alone. But they always left early. We never saw the visitors. To be honest, we tried not to see them. We told you all this before. You keep going over and over it. Leave the damn bone alone, for god's sake."

"How do you know they were women?"

Junior and Pilar looked at each other a bit uncomfortably.

"We heard the sounds," Junior finally said.

"And not of one hand clapping," Pilar added.

"You mean you heard a man and a woman making love."

"Right."

The Didi picture had fallen onto the floor of the carriage. Pratt picked it up and handed it once again to Junior.

"Take another look," he said.

"I'm telling you I never saw this woman in my life."

"I think you're lying," Pratt said. "I think you have been lying all the time. I even think your original statement is a lie." Actually Pratt didn't know what he thought about Junior Walls. He had just decided to see if he could get a rise out of the young man.

But Junior was unmoved. "It's a free country. You think what you want."

"But you heard no lovemaking the night of the murder?"

"That's right. Besides, how could I? Don't you read the papers, Detective? Stuckie was spaced on Nembutal that night."

Pratt fairly hissed at them. "You heard nothing? You saw nothing? You know nothing?"

The young couple did not answer. They sat there grim-faced.

Pratt picked up the photos and placed them in his pocket.

"I will be back here again, my friends," he said.

"And again and again. With the same questions and the same photos."

"How sweet of you," Pilar said.

The moment Rose Vigdor pranced through her clinic door, Didi knew her friend was on one of her weird "natural highs."

It took her about fifteen minutes to snap out of it. All the while Didi was pretending to read a monograph on transitional cell carcinomas of the lower tract in small animals.

Finally Rose grasped Didi's hands in her own and said, "I followed your instructions to the letter. They worked. Not only did they work, but I could have stayed in those places three days and milked all their databases. Not only did it work beyond our wildest dreams . . . not only did they fall hook, line, and sinker for the trumped-up research project . . . but, Didi, I also got one job offer, two sexual propositions, and a promise of a lifetime supply of whatever kind of ground cornmeal I want. Oh, it was, as they used to say, aces! Aces, Dr. N.!"

"Would you like some cocoa?" Didi asked in a calm voice.

"Of course. Of course. I would die for some hot cocoa."

Didi left the clinic area, walked into the kitchen,

and obtained two mugs of Mrs. Tunney's justly famous and complex cocoa.

Mrs. Tunney objected to this kind of activity. She preferred to *serve* her cocoa; to deliver and serve. Didi refused the offer. Even though she realized there would be a price down the road for offending Mrs. Tunney's cocoa protocol. But the old woman got peculiar around Rose. Mrs. Tunney found her so fascinating and inexplicable that she literally circled poor Rose like a researcher about to dissect a frog.

Safely back in the clinic, Didi presented the mug to Rose, who drank greedily. Didi took one or two sips from her own cup and then placed it on the desk. She looked quickly at Rose—thankfully, the manic phase seemed to have ended.

"Now, let's get down to business," Didi said.

Rose whooped. "Don't you understand, Didi? There was no *business*. It was all too easy. Have you used those new ATM machines in the banks? The ones that give you a record of your last five transactions? I mean, poof! Like magic, there it is. In your hand. Well, that's the way it happened. They just pressed a key, typed Rising Moon Farm on the screen, pressed another key, and out came a detailed list of all Rising Moon's purchases during the past six months. It was so easy."

To prove the ease of her task, Rose pulled out

three printouts and laid them end to end on the desk.

"Rising Moon buys most of its feed from Burns and Company. A little from Mappe. And just some weird stuff from Agway."

Didi began to read the list of purchases. Nothing strange here. Nothing revealing here. Just pelleted or ground corn, soybean meal, and assorted grains. And supplements in different forms—vitamins, minerals, trace elements.

Didi felt cheated. Her brilliant scheme had yielded trivial results. This was obviously not the way to gain some understanding of the witch's brew that was being mixed there. A brew that had already claimed the lives of Stuckie and Hiram and destroyed her own reputation.

"As your handpicked assistant in criminal investigation," Rose announced, "I will now evaluate certain of the evidence obtained."

"What evidence?"

Rose picked up the Agway printout.

"What Rising Moon purchased from Agway has nothing to do with pig farming," Rose declared. "So, therefore, these are the purchases that are relevant to the case."

Didi groaned a bit. She grabbed the sheet and reread it.

Rising Moon Farm purchased fluorescent light

bulbs, beef patties, powdered eggs, and condensed milk from Agway over the past six months. Not a lot of each commodity.

"Actually, Rose, very young pigs are given milk in their diets after they are weaned. As for the rest— you're right. Those products don't have anything to do with pigs. And I'm pretty sure they don't have anything to do with the murders. Maybe there was a litter of puppies on the farm. The beef patties and the eggs would make sense then."

"But what about the fluorescent light bulbs, Didi? Aren't they mysterious?" Rose pressed.

"Mysterious? Why?"

"Well, I never was inside Rising Moon Farm, but I've seen it from the outside. And you described it to me. It seems to have been built purposefully to avoid artificial lighting. I mean, there are windows all along that crazy horseshoe. From one end to the other. Every ten feet—from floor to ceiling. It's almost like a stone greenhouse."

"You're right, Rose. Now that I recall, there are no fluorescent lights in either the sleeping area or the pen area. But, remember, Stuckie owned many farms, many dwellings. He could have simply bought them in Hillsbrook and shipped them somewhere else."

Rose nodded and finished the cocoa. "A bust,

then. Nada. It all came to nothing," she said dolefully.

"Don't put it that way. It was a necessary first step," said Didi consolingly.

"Am I fired?"

"Of course not. Not a brilliant grad student like you."

"Thank you. What's next?"

Didi didn't answer. She suddenly thought of Hiram Bechtold. She had a vision of that poor, sick, wonderful old man wandering off into the woods to look for help and finding only his murderer. The image was almost unbearable. She started to weep.

"What's the matter, Didi?" a confused and worried Rose asked.

Didi didn't answer.

"You must drink your cocoa, dear. It's getting cold," Rose said in a scolding, motherly manner. She pushed the mug under Didi's nose, and Didi took it and drank obediently.

She half-choked, coughed, and then slammed the mug down hard on the desk. It sounded like a gunshot.

"Put your arms up! Put your arms up!" Rose counseled, banging Didi on the back.

"Please. I'm fine. I'm fine."

Didi looked at her friend.

"Do you know what Hiram used to say?"

"About what?"

"About when the symptoms were obscure. About when you knew you were in the presence of a sick animal, but for the life of you, you couldn't come up with a rational diagnosis. He said, 'Interrogate the beast.' "

Rose laughed nervously.

"In this case," Didi continued, "he would say, 'Get down in the pen and interrogate the damn pig.' "

"What pig?"

"The pig at Rising Moon Farm."

"But there are dozens of pigs there."

"So there are. Listen, Rose, what are you doing tomorrow morning?"

"Nothing much."

"How would you like to accompany me tomorrow morning on a visit to Rising Moon Farm? As my veterinary assistant."

"But what about Charlie?"

"Oh, I'll give him the morning off."

"Can you just show up there without being called in? Won't it be dangerous?"

"But it's an emergency."

"What emergency?"

"I've been requested by the county agent to check out all pig herds in our area. Because in the north there are disturbing signs of a swine epidemic."

"What epidemic?"

"I'll think of one. I have twelve hours."

"I'm a little frightened, Didi. We are going into the belly of the beast."

"Remember, Rose. Someone there might have murdered Clifford Stuckie—and Hiram Bechtold. But all they did was throw an orange at me. And miss at that."

Charlie Gravis sat back contentedly at the kitchen table. It was nine a.m. Usually by now he was deep into rounds with Dr. Nightingale. He sipped his coffee, chewed on a piece of bread with butter and honey, and smiled.

"Gravis, you're looking mighty pleased with yourself. What is going on with you?" an irritated Mrs. Tunney asked. "And why aren't you out with Miss Quinn?"

"Nothing is going on with me. Nothing at all. Miss Quinn gave me the day off."

"And what are you going to do with all that time?"

"Wait for Trent Tucker. He's going to drive me on . . . on an errand."

"What errand?"

"Nothing big. Just to see an old friend."

"What old friend? All your friends are dead. And the ones still alive won't talk to you anymore."

"That is cruel," Charlie declared.

Trent Tucker appeared just then. "Ready, Charlie?"

Charlie devoured the last morsel and was off like a shot, before Mrs. Tunney could ask any more questions.

Ten minutes later the battered pickup pulled off the road just across from the Hillsbrook High School.

Charlie pointed a finger at the young man. "Now, you listen. I'm going to meet a friend here and have a little conversation. You wait for me in the truck. And keep your mouth shut about this."

Trent Tucker nodded wearily. He was used to getting crazy orders from the old man. Who would care who the old coot was meeting here? Trent flicked the heater switch on. Nothing. In the old heap, heat was an occasional kind of thing.

Charlie climbed laboriously out of the passenger seat side. A figure had emerged from the gym building. It waved in signal to Charlie.

Charlie walked toward it. They met in the center of the windswept teachers' parking lot.

The younger man had that desperate kind of gaze . . . hungry . . . in love . . . reckless.

Yes, Charlie thought. This Newman fellow can

see the future now: young Dr. Quinn in his arms, millions in the bank—freedom.

"I don't have much time. I'm on my break," Ed Newman said.

Charlie didn't say a word. He took out an envelope and handed it to Newman.

"Are these all the numbers?" the teacher asked.

"Not all of them. I figure you needed at least three years' worth of winning Lotto numbers. But all I could get was the past year. Fifty-two weeks' worth. Two games a week. That makes a total of a hundred and four winning number sequences."

"How did you get them?" Newman asked, a bit of skepticism creeping into his tone.

Charlie chuckled. "Wasn't hard. I used Miss Quinn's office phone. It's a push button. See, you—"

Ed Newman interrupted. "Why do you keep calling her Miss Quinn? Her name is Nightingale, isn't it?"

"We all call her that. It was her mother's maiden name. We knew her and loved her. The father, Nightingale, we didn't know at all. Not really. Anyway, as I was saying, I used the push-button phone. I called a toll-free eight hundred number at the New York State Lottery Commission in Albany. You punch in the dates you want. A recording just spits the numbers back at you. As many as you want."

"Was that safe? I mean, someone might have—"

"Hey, Ed. What we're doing is perfectly legal," Charlie retorted in an injured tone. "As for Miss Quinn, she won't know a thing. She don't even bother to check the charges unless the phone bill is way out of sight. And as I told you, these calls were toll-free."

"All right, all right. Anyway, I have one of the computers in school all set up. I'll just feed in the numbers."

"But that ain't enough! We need a formula to make the plays. You come up with that; that's your part, see? You're the damn mathematician."

"No, Charlie. You got it wrong. It's the computer who comes up with it. You just ask the computer for a high probability formula—a model for playing and winning."

Charlie slapped his sides with glee. "Damn, I'd love to be there when you do it. 'Hey, Mr. Computer, give me eight six-number plays for four dollars that will get me eight million dollars.' "

Newman did not pick up on Charlie's glee. He lowered his head and was silent. He seemed to be shivering from the cold.

"Are you sick or something?" Charlie asked.

"No."

"You got to watch your health now, man. Remember, by the time we're ready, the pot is going to be thirty million. Oh, I feel it. I feel it *in my shoes*."

* * *

Didi and Rose arrived at the entrance to Rising Moon Farm at 11:05 A.M.

That was the time she had planned to arrive.

Didi had learned that eleven o'clock in the morning was the ideal time to visit a farming or breeding operation. It was the soft spot in the day; the intense work of the morning chores had been accomplished, but it was too early for lunch. All the workers were lounging a bit. Relaxed. Everyone was relaxed at eleven o'clock.

The day was cold and windy, but the sun was bursting, powerful. It glittered. It burned.

Didi left the key in the Jeep and together with Rose walked slowly toward the two lounging figures in front of the building. All the pickup trucks and other vehicles seemed to be gone.

"Who is that?" Rose whispered.

"The woman is Liz Stuckie, Clifford's sister."

"Who's the other one?"

"That's Herb Donizet."

"The one who stole the jewelry."

"No. That was Ike Flohr. I don't see him. Or his brother, Wilbur. And I don't see Carly Mortimer. But she may be in the house."

"The orange thrower?"

"The very same."

Didi was nervous. She wished she had Allie's support. He was, after all, a cop. Without him, she really was just whistling in the dark. She could theorize . . . she could develop a case like she developed a diagnosis . . . she could even unearth facts and relationships that might be construed as evidence—but without a cop's authority it was meaningless. She knew, for example, that Hiram had been murdered, but she couldn't even discuss the nature of his death with the coroner, or impound his clothes. And because of her rift with Allie, she couldn't persuade him to do so.

She also knew that even if the rift had not occurred, she was dealing with what Allie would call "smoke." Except for that gold key chain, which proved that Hiram Bechtold had spent some time at Rising Moon Farm the night of his death. Or it might have proved that Ike Flohr had been with those vandals who had ransacked Hiram's abandoned vehicle.

Herb Donizet greeted them kindly, saying, "I hope this visit goes better than the last one."

Liz Stuckie grinned at his words. It was, Didi realized, her form of an apology.

She quickly introduced Rose as her assistant, explaining that the woman was filling in for an ailing Charlie Gravis.

Then she went into her carefully thought out veterinary sham. "I need your cooperation," she told the assembled.

"With what?" Liz Stuckie asked a bit harshly. She struck a stiff pose with her lithe body.

"I have been told by the county agent—perhaps 'asked' is a better way to put it—to make on-site inspections of pig herds in the area."

"Why?"

"There has been an outbreak of pleuropneumonia about thirty miles north of here, near Jessupsville. As you know, it can be a severe and contagious respiratory disease."

"Our pigs are fine," Herb Donizet said.

"I'm sure they are. But I'm required to do this when asked. You, of course, have an option. You can call Dr. Treat, your own vet, to make the inspection. It's up to you. But I'm here already, and the whole thing shouldn't take more than twenty minutes."

The foreman and Liz had a silent conference of looks. Liz gave the slightest of nods.

"This way," said Donizet.

Didi stuck out her hand toward Rose. Her assistant gave her the official-looking clipboard with the magnetic pencil attached.

"Just a few questions first," Didi announced, readying the clipboard and the pencil.

"Shoot," said Donizet.

"Any sudden unexplained fatalities in the last ten days?"

"You do mean pigs, don't you?" Liz replied.

Everyone shifted nervously. Was Liz referring to her brother with that flippant question? Or to Hiram? Or both? Was it possible that Liz Stuckie had been close to Hiram? Was that why he had spent time here? Had his connection been with Clifford or Liz or someone else? Was it possible that Liz was grieving for the old professor as much as Didi was?

Didi recovered and stared at Herb Donizet, waiting for an answer to her question.

"None," he said.

"Any of the pigs showing signs of fever?"

"No."

"Anorexia?"

"No."

"Reluctance to move? Thumps? Bloody discharges—nasal or oral?"

"No, none of those."

"Would you sanction serological tests?"

"Not by you."

"Fine. Thank you. Now I have to make a quick site inspection."

"You go right ahead," said Donizet. "Sows and litters in the north wing. Though we have no litters right now. Boars in the south wing."

"Actually," Liz added, "we've shipped most of our stock out."

"Oh? Why is that?" Didi inquired.

"Why does the moon come out at night?" Liz replied nastily.

"Let's go," Didi called to Rose.

The two of them entered the boar wing first and walked slowly down the center aisle. The entire space was flooded with sunlight.

"I never thought a pigpen could be so beautiful," Rose said in wonderment.

"Believe me, this place is unique."

"But look at the floors and the walls, Didi. Why did they cover the stone with tiles? Why didn't they just leave the glorious stone uncovered, like they did on the outside?"

"Stone retains dampness, I guess."

Rose stopped in her tracks in front of a pen. "And who are you? You don't look like any pig I ever saw."

"That's a razorback," Didi said, "probably from Texas or Arkansas. Half wild boar, half domestic pig. The ones from Tennessee are bigger, meaner, and closer to the ancestral European wild boar."

"Well, you look mean enough," Rose said to the bristling hog. He was standing deep in his pen, his bloodshot eyes glaring at them. He had a shorter snout than the domestic pig, and a brownish coat of hair tinged with spots of red. Ugly yellow tusks curved out of his lower jaw.

Didi moved a bit closer, leaning over the fencing. The beast snorted.

"Do you think the lady pigs like someone this ugly?" Rose asked, laughing.

"I would imagine," Didi said, "he's used to impart leanness rather than beauty to a line."

"Well, so long, handsome." Rose blew him a kiss. "He smells like a marsh," she noted.

Didi looked around under the pen. She pointed out to Rose the modern high-tech conveniences, such as the self-regulating water fountain controlled by the hog himself when he wanted to drink, the self-cleaning food troughs, and the artificial mats on the floor of the pen which perfectly mimicked a natural terrain—sand, gravel, brush.

"What are you looking for?" Rose asked as they continued their stroll down the boar wing, stopping briefly at the pens of the three domestic boars who shared the wing with the razorback. All the other pens were empty.

"Signs of infection."

"No, no. I mean really."

"I'm not sure. I'm just looking, period."

Didi halted. She looked about. She felt no sense of threat. She could hardly imagine a malevolent plot being hatched in this spic-and-span place. That was the problem. The midpoint between Clifford Stuckie, Hiram Bechtold, and herself as a Scarlet Woman had to be here. The fulcrum had to be right here. Where else could it be? Suddenly she wondered whether Hiram had come here on that fateful night, and stood in this very aisle, as a veterinarian . . . just as a veterinarian. But that was absurd. Where would Liz have gotten his number if she hadn't known it before? Or perhaps Hiram had merely shown up, the uninvited stranger in a strange land . . . like one of the three Magi.

They moved into the sows' wing, utilizing a narrow hallway that bypassed the living quarters.

"Oh, my God!" Rose exclaimed, not more than two steps into the sows' wing. "There she is! Miss America!"

Facing them, in a pen, was a huge, mature, egg-white Yorkshire sow.

She seemed very happy about the visitors, banging against the side of the pen and making all kinds of delightful grunts and squeals.

"She is a beauty," said Didi, pulling one of the sow's ears gently.

Suddenly Rose put her hand to her mouth in a kind of mock horror.

"I just remembered something terrible," she said.

"What?"

Rose leaned over into the pen and began to point to various parts of the pig, intoning, like a prayer: "Ham, flank, butt, shoulder, hock, loin, fatback."

"Enough!" Didi said. "I remember that butcher's

chart, too. It was probably in every meat store in America."

"Will they make bacon out of her?"

"I doubt it."

Rose leaned over and pulled the sow's other ear. "I never understood why people loathed pigs," she said.

"It's probably because so many cultures used them as sanitation engineers."

"No, it's more than that. It's an unexplained loathing deep in the genes."

"My, my, Rose. Aren't you getting a little carried away?" Didi said, laughing. "Besides, for every two people who hate hogs, there're another two who love them."

"I don't meet those kind of people."

"Well, maybe you don't. But they're out there. People who train hogs to hunt and guard property and carry messages and do all kinds of things from the ridiculous to the sublime, just to prove that hogs are wonderful and smart—even smarter than dogs."

"Are they?"

"I'm afraid they are, Rose. At least, they are if you believe intelligence can be measured by maze solving."

"I'd get a pet pig but I'm afraid the dogs would eat it."

Didi smiled. "A pig can take care of itself. It's tough and smart. Like us, Rose, like us. That's why the pig is getting to be such an important animal in human transplant medicine. It is really very much like us. Same kind of heart. Same kind of circulatory system. And, above all, the same kind of digestive system. Only us and the pigs are so unbelievably omnivorous."

Rose leaned further over the fence. "That's what you are all about, Miss Piggy—flowers and carrion."

Then Rose moved off to check out the other sows in their pens. She seemed on a kind of hog high.

Didi stayed where she was, studying the large Yorkshire, repeating over and over Hiram's advice: When in doubt, interrogate the beast. Talk to the pig.

A wonderful bittersweet memory came to her. Of her last year at vet school in Philly. She was in a bar with several other students and Hiram. The old professor was holding court.

Hiram Bechtold was a specialist in bovine medicine but he had a peculiar passion for hogs. And hogs were his topic that evening. First he started talking about how hogs loved to root. Like humans, he said. We eat potatoes and turnips. We dig tunnels to put our missiles in. We construct subway systems. We love to root, also. And then he talked about how only pigs and humans are so susceptible to so many kinds of flu. Yes, it had been a wonderful evening.

The recent memory of a bitter Gail Bechtold pushed out the fond old memory.

Was that the kind of thing the old woman had hated? Was that what she meant when she hinted that young people had destroyed her husband? Was it a form of geriatric jealousy? How could young people's love for Hiram Bechtold have destroyed him?

Didi looked up. Rose was still meandering. Didi looked down. The big sow was losing interest in her.

"I'm not doing too good a job interrogating you," Didi said to the pig. "This is all nonsense. I should be interrogating Hiram, not you. No hog on the premises is going to tell me why he came here. Least of all, you, Miss Yorkshire."

The sow grunted in assent.

Didi stared down the aisle toward the next sow. She stopped. She had a sudden startling insight into her own stupidity.

Interrogate the beast? Yes. Hiram had always counseled that.

But only if there were no discernible symptoms.

And there was a gross symptom in the murder of Hiram Bechtold, wasn't there?

The vandalized car.

If she was right and he had been murdered, it wasn't teenage vandals who trashed his car.

It was the murderer. And he had been looking for something.

What a fool I have been, Didi said to herself. What an incredible, blind fool.

"Rose!" she yelled out.

Chapter 7

When Pratt was weary he drank rum and Coke no matter the season.

That's what he was drinking on that cold night in a bar in the Kensington section of Philadelphia.

Things were most definitely not going well with him. The Stuckie case was a disaster so far. Nothing. Nada. Except for the love letter, and that hadn't been too productive. Nor had the tentative identification from the clerk at the motel panned out. That hick cop claimed the good Dr. Nightingale had no such clothing—no way.

It *was* Nightingale. He knew it. But he was here and she was there. And the Philadelphia Police Department wasn't going to send John Paul Pratt for an extended vacation in cow country to get her.

He squeezed lemon into the drink. It was, he knew, one of those cases where all the breaks were going against him. Even that old man had gone and died of exposure. The other names on Stuckie's Rolodex had also led nowhere.

The real problem, he realized, was that Clifford Stuckie had long ago cut his ties to the City of Brotherly Love, except for that love nest, the carriage house.

Stuckie had lived elsewhere . . . on one of his farms. The investigator should be in New York or Florida or wherever the hell else the Stuckies had property.

In the middle of his third drink he heard: "You Pratt?"

The voice came from behind. Pratt wheeled on the bar stool. A tall black man with a shaved head and wearing an expensive suit was standing about three feet from him. He was holding an attaché case that probably cost as much as his suit.

"Who wants to know?"

"Don't you remember me?"

"No."

"I'm Rod Lucas's defense attorney."

"I never remember a lawyer's face," said Pratt.

"Can I buy you a drink?"

"No."

"Rod asked me to look you up."

"Isn't he getting sentenced next week?"

"Yes. By the way, my name is Benjamin Bindle."

"That's nice. Now you go and tell your client that,

one, he has nothing to say to me, ever. And two, I hope the judge sinks him in sulfuric acid for forty years."

Pratt turned back to his drink. Rod Lucas was a psycho. This was his second manslaughter conviction. He was one of those characters on the fringe of the restaurant jungle, always showing up as a maitre d' in some suspiciously funded new eatery. Quiet, well-dressed, he would turn into a butcher at the drop of a chef's hat. And that was exactly what he had done this time. Some Puerto Rican busboy had splattered sauce on Rod's fake Armani and Rod had brained him with his own tray. A real sweet guy.

"He has something to trade," said Benjamin Bindle, seating himself on the stool beside Pratt and ordering a rum and orange juice. His drink selection for some reason made Pratt feel a little more kindly.

"It's too late to trade. Too late to plead. Your clown has been convicted. Signed and sealed."

"But not sentenced."

"What's he got?"

"A body."

"Whose?"

The lawyer shrugged.

"Where?"

The lawyer laid his elegant attaché case on the

top of the bar, opened it, and pulled out a soiled square of wrapping paper.

He spread it on the bar in front of Pratt.

The detective stared at the laboriously printed Race Street address. He knew the area well.

There was a childlike representation of a building: a warehouse. Pratt knew it. It used to be an Oriental food wholesaler and before that a Christian mission.

There was a jagged line drawn from the entrance of the building to the third floor rear.

Five containers of some kind were drawn. Two of them had crude stars on them.

"That's all?" asked Pratt.

"That's it."

"Tell him to stuff it!" Pratt said.

The lawyer picked up the paper, folding it carefully, and put it back into his attaché case. Pratt was fascinated with the clicking sound of the case opening and closing.

Benjamin Bindle finished his drink and walked away.

"Wait!" Pratt suddenly called out.

The lawyer was almost at the pub door. He stopped but didn't turn.

Pratt waited. He didn't say another word. Finally the lawyer turned and faced him.

Pratt smiled and shrugged. Yeah, he'd take anything he could get . . . anytime . . . that's why he'd made detective.

The lawyer walked briskly back to the bar.

Charlie Gravis licked the point of his stubby pencil and tested it out on the margin of a week-old local newspaper.

The writing quality was fine. He had long ago lost the beautiful mechanical lead pencil that Miss Quinn had given him as a bonus for good work done.

Charlie felt much better now that he had resolved a moral dilemma—namely, was he being unfair to Ed Newman in the distribution of the money about to become theirs?

He had come to the conclusion that he *was* being unfair and that Ed should get half the winnings.

That would come to about fourteen million dollars each. Hell, he could live with that.

Having successfully dealt with the morality of share and share alike, he realized it was time to lay out a plan that could be put into effect the moment the deed was done. And time was fleeting. The money would be rolling in soon.

Of course, his red Buick was the first priority, but that was really just a necessary indulgence, almost a whim.

Now came the nitty gritty.

He wrote:

BUY SMALL DAIRY FARM AND HERD IN DELAWARE COUNTY.

Then:

SEND ABIGAIL TO MUSIC SCHOOL IN ALBANY. ROCHESTER?

He felt uncomfortable sitting on the edge of his small bed, so he stretched out and propped his back up with the pillows.

An ancient floor lamp curved over the bed and poured down flickering light.

He read over the first two items on his list. He was well-pleased.

Next he wrote:

BUY TWO NEW FORD RANGER PICKUPS FOR TRENT TUCKER.

Yes, he thought, that was brilliant. The only way that good-for-nothing young man would ever earn a living was if he had his own business. And with two new trucks he could start a garbage-hauling service or something like that.

As for Mrs. Tunney, that was difficult. Of course, there were the immediate essentials.

He listed them:

ENGLISH TOASTER

FUR COAT

TEN SESSIONS WITH PODIATRIST

He wet the tip of the pencil again and thought

deeply. If Ed and Miss Quinn moved in together, which was a strong possibility, Mrs. Tunney would feel a bit uncomfortable. Charlie had begun to believe his own fantastical plot.

His face brightened. He knew what he would do for Mrs. Tunney.

He wrote:

BUILD CABIN WITH ALL AMENITIES NEAR PINE FOREST.

He grinned. Yes, that solved the problem.

But, damn! This listing was making him weary. He would have to postpone it for another day or two.

There were also some basics he knew he wouldn't have to list because they would take a while to accomplish.

Such as an endowment to set up a Charles Gravis Chair of Herbal Veterinary Medicine at the state university.

And several contributions to local charities.

He wondered whether he should open a bar and grill with old-style music. But sleep overwhelmed him just as he was formulating a possible menu.

Didi jumped up and muffled the alarm. Then she turned it off. She looked at the face of the clock. Twenty minutes past midnight.

She was already dressed—she had been dressed

for hours—so she walked quietly downstairs, slipped on her parka, and opened the front door just a bit.

Yes! Trent Tucker was sitting in her Jeep.

That was the signal that he had the information. Didi stepped outside, closed the door quickly, and ran to the Jeep.

Once inside, she grabbed him expectantly by the arm. "So you found it!"

"It wasn't hard. They dump derelict cars like that in Fox's lot. Then they auction them off, unless the survivors want them back. Which they never do."

Didi started the engine.

"Do you have the beam?" she asked.

Trent Tucker wielded the huge flashlight like a weapon. She could tell he had been drinking— probably in that rock 'n' roll bar, Jacks.

But right now she didn't care how or where or how inebriated he had been when he acquired the needed information. He had found the car!

It was only a ten-minute drive to Fox's lot, which was located in the Ridge, Hillsbrook's poorest section. The Ridge was dotted with crumbling mobile homes, abandoned trucks, and illegal garbage dumps.

"Is the place accessible?" she asked Tucker. Didi felt as if she were on a criminal mission; that was the reason she had refused to take Rose along.

"What do you mean by that?"

"Is there a security guard?"

"I don't think so. Not at night. They used to have a Rottweiler there. But he caused trouble. They really don't need security. The cars to be auctioned are chained to concrete blocks sunk in the ground. They chain them by the axle."

"What happened to the Rottweiler?"

"They shot him," replied Trent Tucker, who then broke out in crazy laughter that could be explained only by his alcohol intake.

Yes, Didi thought, alcohol surely deranges young men.

When they reached the perimeter of Fox's lot, Didi locked the car and she and Trent marched right through the long, shredded, iron fence.

They were immediately surrounded by a battalion of murdered vehicles, strewn all about. A random, rusting graveyard.

"Do you have a plate number?" he asked.

"No."

Trent Tucker laughed again. "It wouldn't really matter if you did. The plates always get removed. You have a description?"

"I think it's a light green or gray Ford Taurus wagon. A 1992 model."

He flicked on the wide-beam flashlight and they

moved forward. The cars seemed to break the force of the cold wind.

They found Hiram Bechtold's car in about twenty minutes, resting next to a burned-out bakery truck.

Didi went weak in the knees when she saw it.

"Okay," said Trent. "Now tell me what I'm supposed to do."

"Search it."

"What am I looking for?"

"I don't know. Hiram came here to tell me something and to show me something. And then for some reason he didn't. What it was, I don't know. But he was killed for it."

With that in mind, Trent Tucker crawled under the vehicle with the beam.

Didi waited by the right front fender. She didn't lean against the car; she didn't even want to make contact with it. For some reason the car itself had become loathsome.

Trent Tucker explored every inch of the undercarriage. Then he moved to the trunk. Then on to the engine. Finally, the backseat. What had not already been ripped up, he ripped. He literally stripped the backseat away.

But he found nothing.

"If it's not here, it's nowhere," he called out to Didi.

Didi hopped from one foot to the other; the cold

was starting to get to her. She watched him rip apart the wiring under the dash, the floorboard, the glove compartment—everything.

His methodology fascinated her. He seemed to be caught up in an orgy of destruction rather than exploration. It reminded her of the movies she'd seen of those rock bands from the sixties destroying their instruments before the audience's eyes.

Then, suddenly, all his activity stopped. Trent Tucker sat back heavily and threw up his hands.

Didi peered into the car. "Nothing?" she said, wanting desperately to be contradicted.

"Not a damn thing. Either there was nothing here in the first place, or someone got to it before us. Whatever 'it' is."

He slid out of the car and stood beside her. "Now what?" he asked.

Didi did not answer. A wave of sadness rolled over her. Sadness and futility. She had been counting on this. It made sense. It was the first thing in this whole mess that *had* made sense.

"We going home now?" he pressed.

Without answering, she turned and headed toward the Jeep. Trent began to follow her.

"Hey, wait!" he said suddenly.

Didi turned back momentarily. "What?"

"Can I take some stuff from the car?"

"What stuff?"

"You know. The rearview and the steering wheel glove. Like that."

Scavenger, Didi thought bitterly. "Don't you already have a rearview mirror?"

"The one on my truck is shot."

"Oh. Well, okay, I guess. What's a wheel glove?"

"It's that piece of sheepskin around the steering wheel. Old people always put one on because the wheel gets too cold in the winter." He laughed mindlessly. "Old people and hot-rodders."

"Sure," she said wearily. "Go on and take it. Take everything your arms will hold. I'll wait in the car."

She sat behind the wheel of the Jeep, listening to Trent's movements as he tinkered and unscrewed and pushed and pulled.

Didi shook her head ruefully. She didn't understand the scavenger's urge. All that effort over a few worthless items.

Then she heard a short cry. Or was it a shout? Had Trent dropped something on his foot? Maybe he'd had too much to handle and had poked the screwdriver through his own hand.

She went rushing over to him. "What happened? Are you okay?"

He was just fine. No blood, no bumps or bruises.

The cry had been one of triumph. He was standing near the driver's door, grinning.

The powerful flashlight ray illuminated a single

sheet of tightly rolled paper clutched in his left hand.

"It was inside the wheel glove," he declared.

Didi stared at the paper in awe.

The female police officer went first. Her name was Winnifred Born.

Pratt went second.

The other uniformed officer, a male, waited at the ground-floor door of the warehouse, watching both the entrance and the squad car.

Pratt had requested backup not because he was frightened—or even anticipatory—but simply because things had been going so badly. With his luck, he might fall down the stairs, break both his ankles, and die of thirst in this Race Street warehouse.

"There's a nice smell in here," Winnifred Born noted. "What is it?"

"Ginger. Vinegar. And a lot of cleaning chemicals."

Pratt was astonished at how clean the empty warehouse was. Obviously the landlord was trying to keep the property up, hoping the area would come back.

And the residual odor of Asian spices was as oddly pleasing to Pratt as it was to his companion.

"What are we looking for?" Officer Born asked.

"Barrels or containers on the third floor rear."

They found the wide staircase quickly. Officer Born kept her flashlight high, sending showers of light all over, along with the shadows.

It's like being in a fun house, Pratt thought.

He tried to keep his eyes away from the ascending figure of the policewoman; her shapely rear end was just inches ahead of him. She was very attractive. Oh, these black lady cops! Pratt thought. They are too much. They're the only people on earth who can make the uniform of the Philadelphia Police Department look stylish.

"What's in the barrels?" she asked as they reached the third-floor landing.

"Maybe body parts. Maybe chicken soup."

"That's very helpful, Detective," Winnifred Born retorted.

Pratt found her cynical remark very funny. He didn't laugh, however, when he saw the barrels against the wall.

There weren't only five of them, as the lawyer's diagram had led him to believe. There must have been at least twenty.

And they were all overflowing with junk . . . with what seemed to be construction debris.

"Which ones are yours?" Winnifred asked.

"Who the hell knows? Maybe the ones all the way on the left. Or on the right. Or maybe none of them."

Pratt cursed himself for having taken the bait from that lawyer. I had three drinks too many, he reasoned.

"Well, what should we do?" the policewoman asked.

"Here's what we do," Pratt answered, as if after much consideration he had decided on a logical course of action.

It wasn't logical. In a burst of fury he began to kick at the tops of the barrels. He kicked them over. Those he couldn't kick over, he pushed over.

The whole wild, violent thing was finished in thirty seconds.

Then, breathing heavily, Pratt stared down at what he had done.

Officer Born strolled among the debris.

"Well," she said calmly, "you don't have any body parts here. But you do have a body."

All Pratt could do was glare at her.

She shone the flashlight directly on a grotesquely positioned body in a cloudy plastic bag.

"This lady has been dead for a while," she said.

"What's that?" Pratt choked out.

"What's what?"

"That color—that red thing. Shining in the bag."

"Maybe it's bloody clothing."

Pratt waded into the debris. His fingers ripped at the plastic.

It wasn't actually bloody clothing, but the fabric was blood-red in color.

It was the decaying remains of a red brassiere.

Like the motel man had said. Red bra and red panties under a rope dress.

When Allie opened his apartment door and saw Deirdre Quinn Nightingale standing there, he didn't know what to say . . . or do . . . or think.

So he just stood there looking at her. It was past two o'clock in the morning.

"Are you alone?" she asked.

He recovered slightly, enough to answer, "Yeah, sure, except for the three belly dancers."

"Good. Let them stay in bed, Allie. I'll talk to you in the kitchen."

She marched into the kitchen and spread out what seemed to be tissue paper on the old folding dinette table.

"What's up, Didi? What is that and what are you doing here?"

"There's no time for small talk, Allie. Let's just say you got it all wrong."

"Got what wrong?"

"Hiram Bechtold's death wasn't an accident. It was murder. And this is the reason he was killed."

Allie stepped to the table and looked down at the tissue-thin paper.

"What is that?"

"What does it look like?"

"A drawing . . . some kind of crime scene drawing . . . of a corpse."

"Yes, exactly."

"But what are all these marks on the body?"

"The stab wounds on Clifford Stuckie. I think, Allie, that Hiram traced this off the crime scene photo on the coroner's report. I don't know how or where he obtained that, but somehow he did. Don't you see? This must be a reproduction—a map—of the stabbing pattern on Stuckie's body."

Didi rotated the paper slightly so that he would have more light.

"Look at the pattern of the wounds," she urged.

There were many puncture wounds in a large circle, encompassing the nipples on the top and the navel below.

In the center of the circle was another distinct series of punctures—forming a straight line about six inches across.

"Are you looking?" she demanded.

"I'm looking, I'm looking."

"Then you do see the pattern?"

"I see *a* pattern. Yes. But it could be a fluke."

"A fluke?"

"The coroner didn't consider it important. Pratt didn't even notice it."

"You mean this wasn't a purposeful pattern by the stabber?"

"All I'm saying is that a lot of trained people didn't pick up on it."

"Trained people? You mean trained not to see these kinds of things," Didi half shouted.

"Do you want some coffee?"

"Stop trying to change the subject. Tell me what the pattern reminds you of."

He stared down at the drawing for a minute. "Nothing."

"Nothing!?"

"It's a circle and a line, Didi."

"Look harder."

"Well, I guess it looks like some kind of athletic field. Maybe a circular track. And the line in the middle is where they have the field events—like the pole vault."

"No way. It's some kind of mystical symbol. Like a setting sun. Or a rising moon."

Allie shook his head. He checked his pajama bottoms, suddenly afraid his fly was open. Luckily, it wasn't. He said, "Come on, Didi, you're stretching it."

"I'm not. The murderer killed him with a premeditated series of puncture wounds in a premeditated pattern. He had plenty of time to do it.

Stuckie was out on Nembutal. You told me that yourself."

"You read too many books, Didi."

"No, I don't. But Hiram did. He had a whole damn libraryful. He had the largest private library I ever saw."

"So what?"

"So I'm going to Philadelphia because I think I'll find this pattern in his library."

"Do what you want. You don't ask my advice anymore. Remember?"

"I need your help, Allie."

"For what?" he asked bitterly, turning away. He wanted to hold her now. He wanted to kiss her. He wanted the rift between them to be healed on any terms.

"Check out Herb Donizet and the Flohr brothers."

"Check them out how?"

"Whether they've got records, anything criminal in their past. I'm not talking about DWI or taking old jewelry from the farm to pawn when they're broke."

"I'll see what I can do," he said.

She reached up and gently touched him on the cheek. He winced. She brought her arm back quickly, picked up the paper from the table, and ran out.

* * *

The visiting room of Holmsburg State Prison, just north of Philadelphia, was not grim; it had been newly painted in a baby blue.

The folding tables and chairs in the room were of aluminum, and their seats and tops were padded with black plastic.

Pratt slid two packs of Salem cigarettes across the table to Rod Lucas.

"I smoke Newport," the inmate said.

"Bad break for you," replied Pratt.

Lucas opened one pack and lit a cigarette.

"Did you find her?"

"Yeah. Were you the one who did her?"

"Don't be stupid. I've been here for months."

"But you know who did?"

"Not a clue."

"Who was she?"

"Don't know names," Lucas said, blowing smoke toward the ceiling in little waves. "All I know is what she was."

"I'm listening."

"A junkie. A mule. A hooker."

"American?"

"Panamanian."

"Why me, Lucas? Why did your lawyer come to me? There are other guys around with more clout."

Rod Lucas did not answer.

Pratt stared at the man smoking. He really knew why Lucas had picked him; he merely wanted it confirmed. Lucas knew that he was on the Stuckie case. And Lucas knew that there was a connection between the corpse and Stuckie. Oh, yeah, Lucas knew of this connection as sure as he knew his name was Loser.

How did he know? Pratt couldn't figure that. Was it the motel clerk? Had Lucas or one of his associates owned that seedy motel? Who knew?

"Okay. Let's not jerk each other around here, Lucas. What do you want? And what have you got?"

"I know you can't help me out with the sentencing judge," Lucas said.

"So?"

"So there may be some federal charges after I serve the state time."

"For the manslaughter?"

"No. Other charges. And I want them dropped."

"Federal charges need federal people, Lucas. I'm a cop from Philly. You forget that?"

"The ball gotta start rolling somewhere."

"You're going to need a lot, Lucas."

"I have a lot to give."

"Start giving, then."

"I want everything in writing. In my lawyer's hands."

"You get nothing in any way until you give me a

big fat taste of what you got. And it has to be verified by me or my people. Then and only then do you get something in writing."

Rod Lucas nodded in assent. He lit another cigarette. Pratt sat back and waited. It was oddly pleasant here . . . warm as toast.

"Stuckie," Lucas mumbled.

"What? I couldn't hear you."

"Stuckie."

"You mean Clifford Stuckie."

"Right."

"And you have something to give me about Stuckie?"

"A lot."

"Kind of odd that you have a lot about him, Rod. After all, you two traveled in slightly different circles."

"Same circles," he spat out.

Pratt waited for an explanation.

"Money. Same circle. Money's always a circle, isn't it? We both needed it."

"What are you talking about? Stuckie was a millionaire ten times over."

"He needed money."

"How do you know that?"

"Believe me."

"But I don't, Rod."

"He was leaking like a sieve . . . for years. He was leaking on the street."

"Leaking what?"

"Money. What am I talking about here, Pratt—money!"

"What did Stuckie need the money for?"

"That I don't know."

"You're making this up as you go along, Lucas."

"Hell I am. I'll give you names. I'll give you loan sharks in Atlantic City and New York."

"This is all bullshit, Rod."

"I can give you dates."

Pratt stood up. "So long, Rod," he said, and started to leave the room.

"Wait! Okay, okay."

Pratt halted.

"Sit down," Lucas said.

"Only for thirty seconds this time. That's all you have."

The moment Pratt sat down, Lucas leaned over to him. "I couriered for that son of a bitch."

"What are you talking about?"

"I picked up money in New York and brought it to Philly. Large amounts of money."

"What are you saying? You picked up money from Clifford Stuckie in New York? Are you telling me that? Or are you saying that you delivered money to Clifford Stuckie in Philly?"

"I'm not saying either. I said I picked up and de-livered."

"Not from Stuckie."

"No, but *for* him."

"You were told the money was for him? Is that it, Lucas?"

"I was told nothing."

"Then how did you know who the money was from—or for?"

"I knew."

"How often you do this?"

"Twice a month."

"How much money involved?"

"A lot."

"You have to do better than that, Lucas."

"What did I do—count it? A lot. There were bun-dles. Hundreds, fifties, and tens."

"No twenties?"

"No twenties."

"Where in New York did you pick up?"

"In Rockefeller Center, right across from St. Patrick's."

"Who'd you pick up from?"

Lucas went silent. Pratt sighed, leaned over the table, and said, "When you have some names for me, I'll believe you. Otherwise, it's all garbage. Just like that poor dead girl. Sad garbage." He stood again. "Your lawyer knows where to find me."

* * *

Didi was treating the turnpike like her private Grand Prix course. She was driving like a maniac, whipping along the curves, hunkering down on the wheel as if this ride were the most important event in her life.

She made the trip from Hillsbrook to the Philadelphia side of the Camden Bridge in record time.

Gail Bechtold answered the door and stared at Didi.

"Don't you remember me?" Didi asked.

"What is there to remember?" the old lady replied.

"May I come in?"

Mrs. Bechtold held the door open and Didi walked in.

"I came here," she said, "because I have reason to believe your husband was murdered."

Gail Bechtold's laughter sent a chill through Didi.

"Do you mean," Mrs. Bechtold said mockingly, "he didn't just fall, black out, and then freeze to death? Are you saying someone coshed him on the head first?"

"Yes. That is exactly what I mean."

"So what?"

Didi was too stunned to reply.

179

"Did you hear me, young lady? I said, so what? Hiram is just as dead no matter what happened to him. It's over. All over."

They stood together, close, in the hallway.

She must be mad with grief, thought Didi. It was the kind of madness she had seen in cows when their calves were taken away. Not depression but a kind of lunatic high where they eat the strangest things or lash out at pails.

"I'm scrambling some eggs," Gail Bechtold said casually. "Would you like some?"

"No, thank you. I can't stay. But I have a favor to ask of you."

"A party favor?"

Didi ignored the nonsensical query.

"I'd like to look at your husband's library."

"My husband's library? His books? Oh, yes. By all means. Help yourself. Take the books. I don't care. I don't want them."

Then she vanished into the kitchen with a shuffling gait.

Didi climbed the stairs, entered the library, and flicked on the light.

The lushness of it was overwhelming. All those leather chairs and the smell of good bindings.

Surrounded by the books, her confidence suddenly whooshed out of her, like a balloon deflating.

How could she find the key to the stabbing pattern without going through every damn book? It might take days, unless she was lucky and stumbled upon it fast.

But it had to be here. That had to be why Hiram had brought the drawing to her, but at the last minute, for some reason, declined to deliver it. Hiram simply must have come across the design in his reading and remembered the news stories about the multiple stab wounds in Stuckie and then somehow obtained the crime scene photo, in some way, and then put two and two together.

There was no other explanation. Oh, it was a bit far-fetched, but no more far-fetched than a man writing a love letter to a woman he didn't know at all.

She walked over to one wall. Her eyes roamed over the spines.

Yes. These were books that Didi knew. They were Hiram's collection of old veterinary manuals, some dating from the late 1700s.

Hiram used to describe these books as the "Three P's genre—the golden days of veterinary quackery." Purges. Poultices. Prayers. That was the way sick animals used to be treated.

Why not start with these books? She was working blind anyway. Like one of the three blind mice with the other two still unidentified.

She pulled down a fat book from the third shelf

from the top—a late-nineteenth-century textbook on diseases of the dog. The author was Conboy.

Didi smiled. It was a thousand-page tome of which maybe three hundred pages were relevant today, scientifically speaking. Alas, poor Fido. It was very tough in the old days.

She opened the book lovingly to the title page.

Then she laughed out loud.

Stuck in the crevice of the title page, near the spine, was a dollar bill. It obscured the author's name.

No. Wait. Not a dollar. It was a hundred-dollar bill. A crisp, almost new, one-hundred-dollar bill.

She turned to the next page, and then the next.

Another hundred-dollar bill lay nestled in the spine.

Unbelievable!

She inverted the book and shook it vigorously.

A shower of hundreds rained onto the floor, fluttering, diving, spinning like leaves in autumn.

Didi dropped the book to the floor. She selected another one from the shelf at random.

She shook it. Another shower of money. She pulled three more volumes off the shelf. Three more showers of bills.

The floor was soon littered with greenbacks.

She ran to the door of the library and shouted down: "Mrs. Bechtold! Please come up. Now!"

There was no answer.

"Please, Mrs. Bechtold! It's important!" Didi cried, her voice breaking.

Then she heard the older woman slowly climbing the stairs.

Didi ran back to the shelf and plucked another book from it, this one on animal husbandry. She rattled the book. Again the shower of bills.

Gail Bechtold was standing in the doorway.

"Did you call?" she asked calmly.

In her hand was a small bowl and a whisk. In the bowl were three eggs ready to be whipped.

"Do you see this? Look! Look at all this money! These books are filled with hundred-dollar bills."

Mrs. Bechtold looked at the money on the floor of the library. Then she looked at Didi. Then she looked at the shelves.

Finally her gaze returned to the money.

She sighed. "So what?"

"So what!" Didi exploded. "What is going on? Where did this money come from?"

Gail Bechtold smiled.

"Why are you getting so excited, young lady? I thought you'd be happy. Aren't you one of the young people who loved Hiram so much you wanted to make *him* young again?"

"What are you talking about?"

"But I thought you knew. I thought you knew that

your beloved old professor Hiram Bechtold had become a sporting man."

"A what?"

"Oh, yes! He gambled and whored, and last summer he even bought a seersucker suit and a Panama hat."

"Make some sense, Mrs. Bechtold. Please. Listen to me. Did Hiram know a man—a wealthy man—called Clifford Stuckie? Is that where he got all this money? Did Hiram lie to the police when he said he didn't know Stuckie?"

Gail ignored the questions.

"Ah, yes," she said instead. "He was very much the sporting man. That poor, crazy, pathetic, old fool."

She walked to a shelf at the other end of the library.

"And he traveled. Yes, he did. Did you know that? Old Hiram, who taught for forty years in one college, became a world traveler. But you had to know that."

She waited for a reply from Didi.

"No, I didn't know."

"But didn't you want him to travel like a young person?" She took a book from the shelf and held it up. "You see? A travel guide to Mexico. Yes. He even flew to Mexico. Only for a day or two. But he went there."

She dropped the book on the floor like it was a piece of trash. She picked out another one. "And look here. Colombia."

She dropped it and selected another.

"And Venezuela."

She dropped it.

She kept picking up and dropping them, getting angrier and angrier.

"And Peru and Panama and Costa Rica and Puerto Rico and the Philippines and Ecuador."

Then the rage passed and she stood silently, beating the eggs in the bowl.

A phone began to ring downstairs.

Neither of them moved.

The phone went on ringing.

"The telephone, Mrs. Bechtold," Didi said. "Shouldn't you answer it?"

"Should I?"

"Yes. By all means."

Gail Bechtold went downstairs, leaving a bewildered Didi alone among the money and the travel guides.

"It's for you," Gail called up presently.

It had to be Rose, Didi thought. She had given her the number in case Allie dug up some important information.

Didi walked slowly downstairs. It was Rose. Allie

had indeed found something. Didi listened carefully to Rose's recitation.

Allie had discovered that four years ago Herb Donizet was arrested on a breaking and entering charge. It was a warehouse in northern Pennsylvania that had been broken into.

He was loading up a truck with Vitamin K capsules and shots of testosterone in its anabolic steroid form.

That was it. Donizet had been arrested, charged, and sentenced to a fine and three months behind bars.

Then Rose asked if it was snowing in Philadelphia.

No, Didi said.

Rose hung up.

Didi walked into the Bechtold kitchen and sat down.

Gail had just flung the beaten eggs into a sizzling pan.

Vitamin K and testosterone?

Didi didn't understand. Vitamin K deficiency in pigs, the inability to clot fast, was no longer treated by ingesting the vitamin alone. More inclusive dietary supplements were used because vitamins work best synergistically.

And vets never prescribed testosterone in its anabolic steroid form anymore.

Didi laughed nervously to herself.

Wasn't this just another set of bizarre acquisitions by the Rising Moon staff?

There had been beef patties. And condensed milk. And fluorescent light bulbs.

Why not Vitamin K and testosterone?

And why not steal it as well as buy it?

And why shouldn't Hiram Bechtold have become a "sporting man" in his dotage?

After all, most old-time vets gambled. At least a little. It was inevitable, since they earned their bread for the most part from racetracks and dog tracks and the breeders who stocked them.

It had always been so.

The eggs were beginning to burn in the pan.

"Tell me," Mrs. Bechtold said, "did you ever put chile peppers in scrambled eggs?"

"No," said Didi.

"Well, I kept telling Hiram, 'if you're going to places like Mexico, bring me back some fresh-picked chile peppers.'"

"And did he?"

"No. He said it was against the law."

"Is it?" Didi queried, going along with the ridiculous conversation because she was too stupefied to cut it off.

"Of course not; he was lying. But all sporting

men lie, don't they? He didn't bring any back because he was too busy meeting all those people."

"What people?"

"Vets."

"Vets?"

"Of course."

"Please, Mrs. Bechtold. You're making all this up, aren't you?"

The color had drained from Didi's face. Her question was pathetically phrased. She seemed to be begging.

And she was.

For if Hiram Bechtold had really wandered about South and Central America on whirlwind flights, fraternizing with fellow veterinarians, a very ugly scenario was possible.

Didi sat straight up. Her hands squeezed the edge of the table.

And this ugly scenario opened up all kinds of possibilities—and made a lot of the inexplicable clear: from strange purchases and thefts to stabbing patterns; from pig farms that didn't produce litters to hundred-dollar bills falling out of books.

"No," Mrs. Bechtold said happily, moving the scrambled eggs from pan to plate. "I am telling you the truth. Look in his precious travel guides in the library. He has their names and addresses in the margins. Besides, why lie anymore? It's all over, isn't it? I mean, life, you know."

"Am I the only sane person here?" Mrs. Tunney asked.

She sat with Charlie in the kitchen. Breakfast had been prepared and eaten hours ago.

Trent Tucker and Abigail were out doing their chores.

"I don't think so," Charlie Gravis replied.

"Well, it's very clear that Miss Quinn has lost a lot—and I mean a lot—of her marbles."

"Why do you say that?"

"I understand she just up and went to Philadelphia, alone. Left early this morning. And she's been prowling around doing all kinds of things except what she's supposed to be doing—seeing to her practice."

"She sure has been secretive lately," Charlie agreed.

"And as for you, Charlie, you are definitely acting like a crazy old man."

"No, I'm not."

"Yes, you are. You walk around all day with a stupid grin on your face. As if the world was your oyster."

"Just feeling good, Mrs. Tunney. Just feeling good."

"About what?"

Charlie was stumped for an answer.

Then he said, "About everything. After all, we have our health."

Mrs. Tunney gave him one of her patented filthy looks, stood up, and went over to the sink.

Charlie lounged in his chair, staring out the window toward the pine forest.

She will know soon enough why I'm feeling so good, he thought.

Then, right then and there, he had a delicious idea about the fur coat. He would buy it and just leave it at night hanging on the rack in the kitchen where Mrs. Tunney hung her aprons.

When she went down in the morning to start her pot of oatmeal—there it would be.

She reaches for the apron. She picks up a luxurious mink. That would be a humdinger of a surprise. Oh, it would be choice!

Charlie stretched again. He was supposed to cover the office and clinic phones for Miss Quinn while she was away. He would do that. But he was in no rush to man the phones. Besides, he could hear the ringing from the kitchen.

Even though it was still morning and he had had a good night's sleep, he was tired. But this was understandable.

After all, he was due to pick up the numbers from Ed Newman in less than forty-eight hours.

Charlie had his twenty-four dollars safely tucked away. He figured he would have to purchase about forty-eight games, at the most, to win the fourteen million. Probably fewer than that.

It was the anticipation that was making him weary, probably.

But he did feel good. He had the same warm glow he had experienced that one year long ago . . . after he had returned from the war and had spent the next twelve months just drinking, smoking, fornicating, and philosophizing.

A clang hurt his ears. Mrs. Tunney was up to one of her tricks—banging dishes on the edge of the sink, just hard enough to dramatize her disapproval of things but not hard enough to shatter anything.

Charlie sat back and closed his eyes.

Yes, he could remember that year—1946.

He was weary that year, too. But what a glorious fatigue.

Pratt heard his name called out. The bar was crowded now. He didn't turn around. He grinned into his drink.

Here comes that black lawyer again, he thought. Pratt was kind of expecting him. They were going to up the ante.

Pratt had the grisly photograph of the still-unidentified young woman in his pocket. Two photographs, actually. In one, the corpse was still in the bag. In the second, she was out of the bag and her red bra and panties were clearly visible. He wouldn't trade at all with those clowns until he got her name.

When he heard his name called again, he turned toward the sound, because he realized it was a woman's voice.

"What the hell are you doing here?"

"Looking for you," said Didi Nightingale. The seat next to him was taken, so she slid along the bar and stood next to him.

It was awkward for both of them. They stared straight ahead, but they could see each other in the bar mirror.

"No cows in Philly," he noted.

"I don't want to make small talk with you, Detective Pratt. It was too hard finding you. Besides, we really don't like each other."

"I'll buy that," Pratt retorted.

"And we don't have time."

"Can I buy you a drink before you leave?"

"No. And I'd prefer you left with me."

"Is this a sexual proposition?" Pratt asked.

"Sure," Didi replied bitterly. "I want to seduce you so you can write me a love letter."

"Weird sense of humor you have."

"Take a ride with me, Detective. A nice long ride."

"Where to?"

"Hillsbrook."

"For what?"

"I want to present you with the murderers."

"Is that plural?"

"Most likely. Either way, the corpses are plural."

"Who's the second one?"

"Hiram Bechtold."

"I thought the old man froze to death after he got lost."

"What you think and what is the case are two different things."

Pratt laughed. He was beginning to enjoy the repartee. He wondered whether he should tell this arrogant young lady that there was another corpse that might be relevant.

He didn't get the opportunity.

"Did you know that Hiram Bechtold had a large library in his Narbeth home?" Didi asked.

"No."

"Well, he did. And I have just placed an ad in the Hillsbrook paper announcing that I am auctioning his entire library off."

"You're going to truck those books to Hillsbrook?"

"No. I'm not moving a single book. It's just a simple little lie, Detective Pratt, to set a simple little trap."

"They must be very valuable books to someone," Pratt noted.

"Indeed they are."

"How so?"

"Let's just say they contain important information on a criminal organization."

"So he'll grab the books before they are auctioned."

"Grab them or destroy them."

"If you're not crazy, you might be smart, Nightingale."

Then he sat still and pondered the offer. Who was this young woman? Who was she really? He wavered. Should he go to the john and put a call through to that hick cop, Allie Voegler?

"What do you have to lose?" Didi asked.

Pratt shrugged. The lady had a point.

He had been on sting operations that had much less chance of working. And that was what she was really setting up—a long-shot sting.

"Let me sweeten the pot," Didi said, spreading out a piece of thin paper on the top of the bar.

Pratt stared.

"What the hell is that?"

"My, my, Detective. Don't you recognize the stabbing patterns on your favorite corpse's body?"

Pratt felt weak in the legs. Weak in the legs and stupid in the head. He had seen that body, studied it. He had spoken ten times to the medical examiner. He had seen the blood. He had seen the punctures.

But he had never for one moment picked up on the fact that there was a geometric pattern to the wounds.

"I'm ready," he said. He left the drink standing.

Chapter 8

"I don't like this. I really don't like it," said Rose.

She had started to pace in an agitated fashion in front of the large pile of cartons along the south wall of her barn.

The cartons were covered by a tarp. This was supposed to be Bechtold's library. The cartons contained nothing.

"My dogs, Didi. I'm getting frightened. This whole thing frightens me. What if something bad happens? Where will my dogs and I go?"

"Calm down, Rose. Nothing is going to happen. You and the dogs will be staying at my place. Your barn will be covered. Allie will be here. And Detective Pratt. And myself."

She pointed to the two silent police officers standing near the tarp. They looked unhappy but proficient.

"It will be over tonight," Didi promised. "In a few

hours. And then you and the dogs can come right back as if nothing had happened."

"And nothing may happen," Pratt said.

"Do you want me to go now?" Rose asked.

"It would be best," Didi replied.

Rose gathered her dogs. They seemed as forlorn as she.

"Take care of my barn," Rose said to Didi.

"Believe me, I shall."

A half hour later, Rose Vigdor's barn and property were emptied of people, animals, and vehicles.

Except for Didi, Allie, and Pratt. They huddled in the freezing barn around the pathetic stove.

"I can never understand why your friend doesn't run an electric line here and get some damn heat," Allie said.

Didi didn't defend Rose's exercise in natural living. She didn't say a word in response. She was nervous. She was playing an informed hunch and she was playing it over the objection of two men who seemed to be obsessed with her.

Allie Voegler, she knew, loved her but thought she was a scatterbrained, overly intellectual theorist.

Pratt hated her, but thought she was a shrewd bitch.

It wasn't confidence in her, she knew, that had enabled her to enlist their services. It was because they were totally stumped. Pratt, particularly, would grasp at any straw.

But now—right now—to keep them honest and in line, she had to give them something. They were like foxhunting hounds. Sooner or later you had to give them a fox or a bone.

Well, all she could give them now was a bone. The fox was on the way.

She went to her knapsack and returned with one of Hiram's travel guides. It was the only volume she had brought back from his library in Narbeth.

She flipped the pages until she came to a page heavily annotated in the margins with names, addresses, and phone numbers. Then Didi held the book up so that the page was clearly visible to Pratt and Allie.

"This is what they're after?" Pratt asked.

"Right. You're looking at Hiram's contacts in Ecuador. All veterinarians."

"Hell, you can get that data in an Ecuadoran Yellow Pages," Allie noted.

"Only if you know who you're looking for," Didi answered.

"Isn't it time you let us in on the exact nature of this powerful secretive criminal conspiracy?" Pratt asked in a mocking fashion.

"Why don't you do that later?" Allie interjected.

"Shouldn't we just set up this operation? It's getting dark. How do you figure it, Didi?"

"I think he'll cruise by the place a few times. I think he'll be tricked into thinking it's empty. I think he'll leave his car by the road, enter by the barn, confirm that the books in the cartons are Hiram's, and then torch the whole place."

"Makes sense to me," Allie said.

Pratt gave a half nod as if to say that if you accept the premise of the murderer coming here, Didi's scenario is as good as any other.

"So we should take him after he enters the barn and before he goes after the books. If he finds the empty cartons he may get a bit angry and do some harm to your friend's place."

Allie's plan made sense.

"You're the lightest and the youngest, Didi. You take the watch up on Rose's building scaffold. You'll have a clear view of the front. The minute he opens the door to the barn you turn on those battery lanterns and we'll move in."

"No good," said Pratt. "You have to leave that Ecuador guidebook right on top of the carton. You have to wait until he trashes that book and starts looking for the others. You have to take that chance. You have to wait for him to commit himself."

This time, Pratt was making more sense than Allie, and the rural cop agreed. So did Didi.

Allie picked up a blanket and threw it to Pratt. "You wait by the well in the back. I'll be on the far side of the barn. There's an old drainage ditch there."

There was nothing further to say. Darkness was closing in fast.

Didi clambered up the scaffolding and situated herself in a corner where two planks crossed. She held on to a beam with one hand and a rope with the other. It was a long way down.

She could see the road and the front path clearly through the large cracked barn window situated high above the doors like a cathedral window.

Six lanterns stood like soldiers on the board beside her.

It was freezing up there under the rafters. She kept wriggling her hands and toes. Her wristwatch read five o'clock. Whatever was going to happen would happen early, she figured. The intruder would look the place over as soon as it got dark. Time was precious for him, too.

Up there, alone, Didi realized there were only two possibilities: Either she was the biggest fool in Christendom or she was one smart vet who had put two and two together when no one else could.

At five-thirty she started to sing Patsy Cline songs softly to herself.

At six she began to hum the hymns her mother had sung while cleaning the house.

At six-thirty she started to recite the lines from her high school play, *Julius Caesar.* She had played Brutus, dressed in a motorcycle jacket, because the drama society had run out of boys.

At seven o'clock she saw car lights. Moving slowly.

They vanished. They returned. They vanished. They returned. The same lights. The same car.

She felt a flush of heat in her face. One leg cramped.

The little car stopped just outside the property and the driver shut the lights off.

Didi pulled the lanterns closer. Her heart was beginning to thump like a sheepdog's when it sees its first flock.

A tall, lithe figure emerged from the car. He was wearing a ski mask and a work jacket.

He began to walk very slowly toward the barn, like a stalking cat: one step, and stop; then two steps, and stop.

Now he was only thirty feet from the barn entrance.

Didi crouched on the beam, waiting for him to complete the journey . . . to push open the barn door.

She felt a strange affection for this murderous intruder. She knew why, and it embarrassed her. He had confirmed her wisdom by taking the bait.

But this time he didn't move again. He just stood there and looked.

Didi was silently urging him forward.

Still, he stayed put.

Then he did a strange thing. He unzipped his jacket and pulled something out.

Two objects, in fact. He held them both in his left hand, then with the right hand pulled out a smaller object from his pocket.

Didi saw a flicker of light.

And then suddenly she saw the two objects ignite.

And the intruder brought his arm back.

At that moment Didi knew she had made a terrible mistake.

The stranger was not here to selectively winnow out dangerous books. He was going to burn the whole barn down and make sure.

A moment before he released the two Molotov cocktails, Didi flung the first lantern at hand through the barn window.

Then she clambered down the makeshift ladder and ran outside, screaming to Pratt and Allie, removing her coat as she ran.

One of the flaming bottles hit a barn door and ignited. The other fizzled, fell, and neither shattered nor ignited.

Didi beat the small flames out with her coat before they could spread. Then she turned and walked slowly to the intruder.

He was lying facedown on the ground. Pratt held a gun to his head. Allie was just finishing cuffing him.

Didi, breathing heavily, her face blackened from the fire grit, felt nothing but hatred now for this individual who would destroy her friend's home.

She bent down and savagely ripped the ski mask off.

Then she staggered back.

It wasn't a man.

It was a young woman.

A fair-skinned black woman—or a dark-skinned white woman.

And Didi had never laid eyes on her in her life.

Pratt whistled low. "I'll be damned."

"Do you know her?" Didi demanded.

"I sure do. Her name is Pilar Walls. She's married to the caretaker of Stuckie's carriage house in Philadelphia."

Didi recovered her poise. She crouched down beside the young woman.

"Who sent you?" she asked.

Pilar was silent.

"Who murdered Clifford Stuckie?"

The girl didn't say a word.

"Look, I know you're involved. But I don't think you're a murderer. Who killed Hiram Bechtold?"

Still no response from the young woman.

"Don't be a fool. Save yourself. Tell us."

Not a sound came from Pilar. She seemed to be in a kind of self-induced trance.

"It doesn't look like you'll get anything out of her," Allie said.

"She'll talk when she realizes I know what the whole thing is about. She'll talk when we take her to Rising Moon Farm and show her the truth."

"You mean now?"

"Yes, now."

"What are you talking about—just barging in at that pig farm with all those people there?"

"There won't be anyone there, Allie. They'll be out, in a large restaurant, so that all of them can be seen together, to solidify their alibi. Because they sure as hell sent this Pilar to destroy Hiram's notes. Remember, I placed the auction notice in the Hillsbrook paper, not in Philadelphia."

"I hope you know what you're doing, Didi," Allie cautioned.

"Oh, I do. And stop calling it a pig farm."

She turned to Pilar.

"Tell my friends what that place really is."

But Pilar remained stonily silent.

"It's like that television series, isn't it? *Upstairs/ Downstairs*. Upstairs is one world. Downstairs another."

"There is no downstairs or upstairs in that building. Make sense, Didi. I've seen the place."

She laughed, a manic, exhausted sound.

"We'll take her car!" Didi shouted. Neither Pratt nor Allie objected. They picked the young woman up and headed for the small GEO parked on the road.

Didi drove boldly up to the front door of Rising Moon Farm. Then she braked sharply, as if braking were meant to be a provocation.

The lights in the living quarters were blazing.

Pratt said, "I thought you assured us they would be in a restaurant."

"They are," Didi replied. "You just don't know country etiquette. In Philly, when you go out for the evening you shut all the lights and lock all the windows and doors. In Hillsbrook, you turn on the lights and leave the doors and windows open."

"I don't care how open those doors are, Didi. We can't just walk in there looking for contraband," Allie insisted.

"Contraband? Who said anything about contraband? I'm talking about a criminal conspiracy that has already taken two lives."

"So you say. The fact of the matter is, Didi, that we can't just go in there without a warrant."

"The way I see it," Pratt said, "we have reason to believe that this lady, this Pilar Walls, has placed incendiary devices on the premises of Rising Moon Farm. And since we caught her in the process of using said incendiary devices against another farm, we are within our rights to enter and search. It is a question of public safety."

Didi found that exposition funny. "Bring her along," she said, pointing to the still-silent Pilar. "This whole exercise is for her benefit. She's going to find out we know quite a bit. And I'm going to give you gentlemen a tour."

She entered the building as if it were hers. There was no one about . . . no one home. All the lights had been left on, including the hallway lights, which seemed to flood the adjacent pens.

"We are entering the sow wing," Didi announced to those trailing behind her. "Notice the lovely tiles on the walls."

She stopped in front of Miss Piggy, her old Yorkshire friend, who was grunting up a storm.

"Isn't it strange to have tiles like this in a pigpen? They're usually used to soundproof an area. But pigs don't make much noise. And notice you don't see any fluorescent light fixtures here. But Rising Moon kept buying fluorescent light bulbs. And look in the feed trough, gentlemen. You won't see any beef patties or condensed milk or Vitamin K pellets or testosterone Syrettes. Pigs don't use them. But Rising Moon Farm purchased all of that—or stole it. Aren't I right, Pilar?"

No one responded to Didi. Allie looked around nervously.

"Like I said," Didi continued, "Rising Moon Farm has an upstairs. We are in it. A pig farm. But there's also a downstairs, and they don't raise pigs there."

Then Didi leaped lightly over the fence and into the pen with Miss Piggy.

"And I think the way to go through the looking glass is in one of these pens. Under the mats that simulate gravel and brush. And I think, in fact, it's right here in Miss Piggy's garden. This little piggy gets to guard the keys to the kingdom."

Didi began to roll up the mat on the floor of the pen.

Miss Piggy charged, knocking into her and sending Didi sprawling.

Allie leaped over the fence, his gun drawn.

"Put that stupid thing away!" Didi shouted as she scrambled to her feet.

It didn't take long for the white sow to lose interest in the proceedings. She turned her back on the human doings.

Didi knocked the debris from her clothing. "I'm fine. Help me with this, Allie."

Together they began to roll up Miss Piggy's flooring.

"Well, I'll be damned!" Allie exclaimed. "This is getting to be like a version of *Treasure Island*. Is Long John Silver going to pop out?"

Smack in the center of the pen was an old-fashioned stone door with a brass handle.

"Like a root cellar," Didi said.

They pulled it open and walked cautiously downstairs on the thick wooden steps.

They moved in single file. First Didi, then Allie, then Pilar Walls, still cuffed, then Detective Pratt.

The fluorescent lights ran the entire length of the downstairs. And the lights were on.

"It's a damn poultry operation," said Allie, pointing to the mass of electric incubators, electronically controlled brooders for chicks, and the many small cages and runs, all empty.

Didi bent down and picked up some floor pebbles. She smelled them. Ground oyster shells and charcoal. She smiled. Old-fashioned digestive aids for a creature that was fed beef and milk and dosed with Vitamin K and testosterone.

"Not the kind of poultry you're thinking of, Allie," she noted. She turned to Pilar. "Is it?"

Then Didi's eyes caught a covered cage down the aisle. She walked there quickly and pulled the cloth off with a savage jerk.

"Behold!" she said triumphantly.

In the cage, staring out, was a beautiful rooster. His long wings were tinged with vermilion. Vermilion-tinged also were the feathers on head and thigh. The high curving tail was peacock blue, and he had a savage lemon beak and orange feet and legs.

He was a magnificent five-pound package of restrained fury.

"That's no barnyard rooster," Allie whispered. "That's a fighting cock."

"He may have been once. But no more. Look at his comb and wattles. They're not clipped for fighting. This one's a stud."

"So what *do* we have here, Didi?"

"A very large breeding operation for fighting cocks. Secret, high-tech, and larger than anything I ever heard of before."

"But cockfighting is illegal in New York and most northern states," Allie said.

"They ship the birds south."

"Georgia? Florida?"

"No. There's no money in U.S. cockfighting. Here, it's a poor man's sport. But in South America that's all changed. Drug money changed it. Twenty thousand dollars for an undistinguished fighting cock is quite common now. And the betting is wild . . . it goes into the millions.

"Even more interesting, for some reason down there——in South and Central America—veterinarians control the sport. They own the cockfighting rings. They manage them. They define the rules."

Didi stared at the brilliantly colored gamecock in the cage.

"And that's what was carved into Clifford Stuckie's chest. The perimeter of a cockfighting ring—a circle. And the line in the middle of the circle was where they 'pit' the cocks before the fight. They let them peck at each other, held by their handlers, to get them riled up for the main bloody match.

"I don't know how Stuckie and Hiram got together. But it was obviously Hiram who made the contacts with the South American vets. And the money probably changed hands through him. I don't know who brought the cocks they bred here down south.

"And I don't know who murdered Stuckie . . . or why. But the killer must have wanted to make an additional poetic point. The murder weapon was obviously gaffs—sharpened steel points that are attached to a fighting cock's legs so that he can punc-

211

ture the opponent until he dies from shock or loss of blood."

Allie asked, "Why would a wealthy man like Stuckie go into something like this?"

"Maybe he wasn't so wealthy anymore. Or, more likely, he was one of those men who become obsessed with breeding. Particularly breeding some kind of killer strain. That vet, Louis Treat, hinted to me that Stuckie was that sort of man."

Didi looked over at the would-be arsonist. "Pilar can tell us what we don't know."

But Pilar kept her head down—still silent.

"Don't worry," Pratt chimed in. "Pilar is going to tell us everything in a few minutes."

The detective had a very strange look on his face.

He began to circle the young woman.

"What are you going to do? Beat it out of her?" Didi asked acidly.

Pratt snorted. "These bright lights," he said, "are wonderful. I've never seen her in such a light before."

Then he put his leering face close to Pilar's. She winced.

"Yeah," Pratt said, "I think I met someone who looks very much like you. Close enough, in fact, to be your sister."

He reached into his pocket and pulled out an envelope. Then he extricated two photographs and let the envelope flutter to the floor.

Pratt held the photos up close to Pilar's face.

Her eyes grew wide with horror. "Oh, my God! My God, it's Davida! Davida!" she shouted in gasps, as if she could not draw enough breath.

And then she began to scream and rant. She fell to her knees, sobbing.

"Get those handcuffs off her!" Didi called out.

Pratt knelt beside the hysterical girl. He stroked her head. The bad cop had turned into the good cop.

"She was your sister, wasn't she?" Pratt asked, tapping the death photos of the scantily clad young woman found in the plastic bag in the Race Street warehouse.

Pilar nodded, over and over again.

Finally she was able to speak again, but in a trancelike monotone. "Yes, it's my sister. It's Davida."

"Why would they kill her?"

"I don't know."

"Why was Stuckie killed?"

"Because he had squandered all the money. Because he told his sister Liz that breeding the cocks would make their family wealthy again . . . that they'd be able to pay off all their debts." She looked at

213

Pratt alone as she spoke, as if he had hypnotized her.

"But they didn't . . . did they?"

"No. Clifford couldn't stop gambling. My sister delivered the birds. She knew the drug dealers. She and the old man brought back the money. There was a lot of money. But it vanished. Anything you gave Clifford Stuckie vanished—money, land, people."

She began to rock, her eyes seeking out and then being repelled by the horrendous picture of her sister's corpse that Pratt had conveniently placed on the floor in front of her.

Allie brought her a cup of water and removed the cuffs from her wrists. She coughed the water up between sobs. She looked around now for some kind of help; none was forthcoming.

"Did you kill Clifford Stuckie, Pilar?" Didi asked.

"No. No. No," she half screamed, scrambling to her feet.

"They slaughtered your sister like a pig," Pratt said nastily. "You owe them nothing, Pilar. Nothing."

"I didn't know they were going to kill Clifford. They told me to open the door—the front door of the carriage house—after he arrived. And then to just go back to bed. I didn't know they were going to kill him."

"Who ordered you to open the door?"

"Liz. Liz Stuckie."

"Who came into the carriage house?"

"Donizet. Herb Donizet. He's the one who came in after I unlocked the door."

"Did Donizet also kill the old professor—Bechtold?"

"I don't know."

"Why did they kill the old professor?"

"I don't know anything about that. I swear."

"Take a guess."

"Maybe because he didn't want to be involved in Clifford's murder. Maybe he had something that proved the orders for Clifford's murder came from his own sister. Maybe he just had enough and wanted out and was threatening to expose the gamecock schemes. I don't know, I told you."

"Why do you think they killed your sister?"

She looked for a moment as if she were going to attack John Paul Pratt. Then she balled her hands into fists and began to pound them into her own stomach. She shook her head piteously.

"Who knows?" she wailed. "Who knows why they would want to kill Davida. They were killing everyone, weren't they? But I think it was because Clifford Stuckie loved her. Liz had begun to believe that her brother was a devil destroying them all with his passion for gambling and breeding. My sister was sleeping with him. Sleeping with the devil."

"What about Carly Mortimer, Stuckie's so-called fiancée?"

"She wasn't in it. She was too stupid to realize who she was dealing with."

"So your sister . . . Davida . . . she was the 'D' in the letter Stuckie was writing."

"Yes. I found the letter. I wanted to protect her. Clifford kept a lot of old envelopes and checks and bills in a box in the phone closet. Stuff he was supposed to send out and never did. Or bills that had received duplicate payment because he had no accounting sense. I found a check in an envelope that was supposed to have been sent a long time ago to a Dr. Nightingale. Her first name was Deirdre. I ripped the check up and placed the envelope next to the letter. I never even noticed the envelope had the old postage rate."

"Who ordered you to burn the barn tonight?"

"Liz Stuckie."

"How much was she to pay you?"

"A thousand dollars."

"Did your husband know of your involvement with the Stuckies? Or your sister's?"

"Junior knows nothing except music."

Inexplicably, since it was not dawn, the fighting cock in the cage began to crow.

Didi shivered. Allie took her hand.

Detective Pratt gathered the photos, replaced

them in the envelope, and shoved it into Pilar's jacket pocket.

They could all hear Miss Piggy grunting at the top of the stairs.

Yes, Charlie thought, sitting behind the wheel of Trent Tucker's ancient pickup—yes, this is the way it should be.

A clandestine meeting on a bitter winter night.

Of course, they were doing nothing illegal. But they sure were doing something exciting.

The meeting place had been selected by Charlie: a twisted lane north of the Ridge . . . local hunters knew it as a deer crossing.

He lit a cigar. The ash glowed. The heater wasn't working.

He checked his watch. Newman was due in three minutes; a hundred and eighty seconds. He closed his eyes and started to count down.

Newman showed forty seconds early. He pulled his car right up next to Charlie's, pointed the other way so they would be driver's window to driver's window.

The younger man smiled as he rolled down the window.

"You got it?" Charlie asked.

"Signed, sealed, and about to be delivered," Ed replied.

He handed Charlie a rolled-up sheet of computer paper.

Charlie grabbed it and unrolled. But the damn cab light wouldn't work. He tried puffing furiously on the cigar to use the lit end as a beam—but it was too dim.

Finally, he climbed out of the pickup and walked into Ed Newman's headlights.

He stared at the long sheet of paper.

All he felt at first glance was a kind of sinking weakness—like liver trouble.

And then he let out a bellow of geriatric rage and strode over to Ed Newman's open window.

"What the hell is this, Ed?"

"Calm down. What's the matter?"

"Look at this!" Charlie yelled, shoving the paper in his face.

"Charlie, calm down! Please! These are the winning combinations."

"There are thousands of combinations on this list, Ed."

"That's right. Thirty-six hundred six-number combinations. The computer identified all thirty-six hundred as the ones to play in order to guarantee a winner in the next Pick-6 Lotto drawing."

"Ed, that's thirty-six hundred individual games! That's eighteen hundred dollars! Do you have eighteen hundred dollars?"

"No."

"And who'd fill out all the tickets? We'd have to hire a damn army."

"I did what you asked, Charlie. Exactly what you asked."

Charlie didn't say a word. He staggered back to the cab and climbed in.

He looked up at the night sky. He could see the fourteen million dollars flying away, like a shooting star.

Charlie stared at Ed Newman again. The younger man looked dazed.

Well, Charlie Gravis thought, Ed Newman really is not Miss Quinn's kind of fellow. She really needs a sporting man. Deep in Deirdre Quinn Nightingale's heart, that was the kind of man she hankered for. Charlie just knew it.

Ah, but he was much too old for her.

It was only a mile and a half from Deirdre Quinn Nightingale's property to the abandoned piece of land called Lubin's Field.

But it took the procession a full hour to make the trip.

And what a strange procession it was on that late Sunday morning, one week after Easter.

At the front of the column, like General Sheridan, Deirdre Quinn Nightingale, D.V.M., rode her horse at a stately pace.

Stretched out behind her were all her troops— her "elves," as she called them—the permanent residents she had inherited from her mother along with the land and the house.

Behind Didi and her fine horse, Promise Me, walked elf number one: old Charlie Gravis, her veterinary assistant. He was leading Sara, a Spotted Poland China sow.

Then came the acerbic Mrs. Tunney, the "house-keeper" of the Nightingale home. She carried two of Sara's piglets in a large wicker basket.

After Mrs. Tunney came young Trent Tucker, driving his battered pickup truck at a snail's pace.

And in the open back of the truck sat Abigail with four of the yard dogs—four being as many as she had been able to round up. The numberless barn cats had eluded her altogether. She had failed to corral even one of them.

The dogs howled and moaned and never gave up trying to jump out of the truck bed. But Abigail patrolled the perimeter resolutely, gently pulling them away from the edge.

Didi was not enjoying herself. She found the whole thing rather ridiculous.

The procession was going to Lubin's Field because that was where the blessing of the animals would take place. The ritual was cosponsored by two churches in Hillsbrook, neither of which Didi—nor any of her elves—belonged to.

Anybody who had a farm animal or a pet was urged to bring it to Lubin's Field, where the ministers would bless the dear beasts en masse.

This was the second such festival in Hillsbrook. It was patterned on the justly famous annual rite at the Church of St. John the Divine, in New York City, which attracted even elephants.

Didi had ignored requests by Mrs. Tunney and Abigail to attend the ritual last year, but this year the two of them had been so persistent they wore her down.

In a moment of weakness, she had agreed.

And here she was. Unhappy. Feeling foolish. To her mind the creatures of the earth were born "blessed." Additional ministrations were unnecessary. Even excessive.

The moment the field was visible, Didi climbed down from her horse and held the reins in her hand tightly.

Promise Me was a bit frightened, she could tell.

The field was literally a carpet of beasts and their proud owners.

There were goats, sheep, calves, workhorses and riding horses, dogs and cats without number, birds in cages and parrots on shoulders. There were many exotic beasts, also: from boas to llamas to glass-encased scorpions.

And there were children . . . so many children. Enough for a new-style, sneaker-wearing Crusade.

The dairy farmers had obviously taken a pass on the festival. Only five or six dairy cows were present, placidly looking over the throng, oblivious to the fretting babies and the general cacophony. As Didi had noted so many times in the past, dairy cows, for whatever reason, were virtually fearless.

A sturdy wooden stand had been constructed in the center of the field—the altar—and the structure was ringed with sound equipment.

Didi could see Father Jessup and Reverend Arlo already on the stage.

Also onstage was John Breitland, head of the Hillsbrook chapter of the Dutchess County Animal Welfare League.

Breitland was the last surviving member of the once-wealthy and socially prominent Breitland family, manufacturers of dairy equipment.

Their company had gone bankrupt in 1973. There was nothing left of the Breitland fortune but a large house and twenty-one hundred of the most beautiful acres in Hillsbrook. John Breitland lived in that house alone. He was only forty-one years old, but he was treated with the kind of deference accorded to a powerful patriarch. Even those neighbors who had known him all his life called him Mr. Breitland—the influence and prestige of the family name still being strong.

Didi guided her contingent to an empty space to the left of the portable stage.

Practically all the assembled were neighbors and friends and business acquaintances. Everybody seemed to know everybody else and there was much nodding and waving in greeting. There was little conversation, however, because the animals to be blessed had to be watched and controlled.

One slipup, and a chain reaction could turn Lubin's Field into a land of chaos. One dog could nip one horse who would then kick out at one cat who would dart away and scratch the nose of one sow while fleeing—and, well, the possibilities were endless.

Didi drove a sharp wooden stake into the ground and tethered Promise Me to it.

Trent Tucker parked the truck perpendicular to the horse, and Charlie then tied the big sow to a wheel axle with a frayed rope.

Mrs. Tunney deposited the piglets beside her.

Abigail stayed in the open back of the truck, tending the yard dogs, who now were greedily surveying the other dogs in the field as if they couldn't decide which one to attack first.

"Look! The mayor!" Mrs. Tunney called out in a hoarse stage whisper.

Sure enough, Lila Caro, the mayor of Hillsbrook, was walking swiftly toward the wooden stage.

She was a tall woman with bristling gray hair that stood up all around her head like a cactus. She always wore farm work clothes and carried a clipboard.

Her husband had started the first successful bakery in the Hillsbrook area. When he ran off with a young stable girl, Lila had shut down the bakery and gone into politics. There were rumors that she was about to seek state office.

"If she's going to bless our pigs," Charlie said, "we might as well turn them into pork chops now."

"That is a terrible thing to say," Mrs. Tunney chastised. "She is the best mayor this town has ever had."

"And I'm Winston Churchill," Charlie retorted.

"At least she cleaned out the crooks."

"What crooks? She's been in office for two years. She found one pathetic character who'd bribed somebody on the zoning commission. And it may not even have been a bribe."

"Face it, Charlie Gravis. You can't stand the idea of a lady mayor."

"I don't like a blind lady mayor."

"You don't have to see in this town. All you have to do is smell."

Didi saw a political battle royale brewing, so she stepped right into the breach. "Did you bring that thermos, Mrs. Tunney?"

Before Didi could get her answer, applause erupted behind her, drowning out Mrs. Tunney's response.

It was Burt Conyers striding through the crowd.

The applause was a bit ironic and a bit derisive. Conyers was a certified eccentric. He went about in all seasons in the same sheepskin vest and sneakers and bamboo cane.

He had always proclaimed himself a poet, but no

one in Hillsbrook believed him until an Albany public television station did a program on him and declared him to be an important rural poet in the Robert Frost tradition.

Since then, as a local literary celebrity, he was always invited to invocations and convocations to open the ceremonies with a poem.

As for the poetry itself, it had a macabre pastoral bent. His work was usually about roadkill or diseased trees or rutting deer or mushrooms as phallic images.

The moment the poet reached the wooden platform and negotiated the steps up to the stage, Mayor Caro walked to the pulpit.

Didi rubbed Promise Me's nose. The big horse had settled in quite happily.

Didi felt a tug on her sleeve. It was Mrs. Tunney handing her the thermos. She unscrewed the top, poured some tea into the cup, and drank. It was good. Lots of honey and lemon.

What a glorious day it is, Didi thought, looking at the bright blue sky, with its single swath of clouds, and the woods past the field.

She rescrewed the top and handed the thermos back to Mrs. Tunney.

Mayor Caro's speech was short, sweet, and nonpolitical. She simply welcomed the people and the animals, then sat down on one of the folding metal chairs arrayed onstage.

The poet approached the pulpit.

Didi's cynicism was beginning to vanish altogether. She was beginning to feel a sense of strong community with all her Hillsbrook neighbors and their beasts in that field. She was beginning, in fact, to feel elated.

But where was her good friend Rose Vigdor? she suddenly thought.

Didi looked around. Ah! Rose and her three dogs were about a hundred yards away.

Rose was lying blissfully on her back. Huck, the Corgi, was chewing happily on one corner of the blanket. The two German shepherds, Aretha and Bozo, were sitting alertly, side by side, watching the stage, obviously waiting anxiously for the blessing, or perhaps a dog bone.

Didi laid her head against Promise Me's neck. For all she knew, her horse, too, was anxious to be blessed. One thing Didi had learned as a vet was that the mind of a horse is bewildering and unfathomable.

Burt Conyers started to recite his poem. He fairly shouted it, reading from a single sheet of paper that he had smoothed out on the pulpit.

> *Behold the wildflowers*
> *Those sweet carpets of death.*
> *Suck in their sweet strychnine pollen!*

Oh, my! Didi thought. He's not going to lighten up, even this morning.

She tuned him out and stared at the sky instead. A V formation of geese was moving very high and very fast. Going home.

Suddenly Didi had one of those strange intuitions: she was being watched . . . stared at.

It was a very strong intuition.

Slowly she turned her head.

She found the source, and groaned.

It was Carswell, the beagle. He was standing about twenty yards from her—staring. Ears up. Tail up.

She looked around desperately for Mrs. Niles, his owner. But she was nowhere to be seen.

Carswell had never forgiven Dr. Nightingale.

About a year ago he had chased some critter through barbed wire and cut himself badly. The wounds had become infected. Didi had treated the beagle successfully, but for some reason the local freezing agent she had used as an anesthetic had not worked very well. Carswell blamed her for his suffering, as well he might, although he had got into his own trouble. He would set upon her or her red Jeep anytime he caught sight of them—anywhere. Two of the attacks occurred in town, one in the cleaning store.

There was no time now to plan an escape.

The beagle launched his attack with a barely audible yip and ran toward her, low to the ground.

Sweet Abigail of the golden tresses, or dim-witted

Abigail, as some people called her behind her back, saw the charge and released one of the yard dogs, nicknamed Ironhead, to blunt the attack.

The two dogs walloped into each other not more than five feet from Didi. They were soon joined in combat.

The fight ended quickly, however. Before it ever really got going.

A terrible sound splintered the morning air.

There was a *crack*! And then an echo.

The dogs stopped scrapping immediately. Every living thing—human and beast—froze in place.

This was hunting country. Everyone in Lubin's Field knew the sound of a high-powered bullet fired at close range. In clear weather.

Didi looked up at the makeshift wooden stage.

The poet was standing. The ministers were standing. The mayor was standing.

Only John Breitland was lying on the wooden planks.

The bullet had entered his right eye and blown his brains out onto Father Jessup.

Eyes bulging, Father Jessup remained as he had been, a cry caught in his throat.

Burt Conyers decided to finish his poem. But the unblessed beasts and their protectors were already fleeing Lubin's Field.

Explore the intriguing
world of
Dr. Deirdre Quinn Nightingale
in these exciting
mysteries from Signet

DR. NIGHTINGALE COMES HOME

Deirdre "Didi" Quinn Nightingale needs to solve a baffling mystery to save her struggling veterinary practice in New York State. Bouncing her red Jeep along country roads, she is headed for the herd of beautiful, but suddenly very crazy, French Alpine dairy goats of a "new money" gentleman farmer. Diagnosing the goats' strange malady will test her investigative skills and win her a much needed wealthy client. But the goat enigma is just a warm-up for murder. Old Dick Obey, her dearest friend since she opened her office, is found dead, mutilated by wild dogs. Or so the local police force says. Didi's look at the evidence from a vet's perspective convinces her the killer species isn't canine but human. Now she's snooping among the region's forgotten farms and tiny hamlets, where a pretty sleuth had better tread carefully on a twisted trail of animal tracks, human lies, and passions gone deadly. . . .

DR. NIGHTINGALE RIDES THE ELEPHANT

Excitement is making Deirdre "Didi" Nightingale, D.V.M., feel like a child again. There'll be no sick cows today. No clinic. No rounds. She is going to the circus. But shortly after she becomes veterinarian on call for a small traveling circus, Dolly, an extremely gentle Asian elephant, goes berserk and kills a beautiful dancer before a horrified crowd. Branded a rogue, Dolly seems doomed, and in Didi's opinion it's a bum rap that shouldn't happen to a dog. Didi is certain someone tampered with the elephant and is determined to save the magnificent beast from being put down. Her investigation into the tragedy leads her to another corpse, an explosively angry tiger trainer, and a "little people" performer with a big clue. Now, in the exotic world of the big top, Didi is walking the high wire between danger and compassion . . . knowing that the wild things are really found in the darkness, deep in a killer's twisted mind.

DR. NIGHTINGALE GOES TO THE DOGS

Veterinarian Deirdre "Didi" Quinn Nightingale has the birthday blues. It's her day, and it's been a disaster. First she's knee-deep in mud during a "bedside" visit to a stud pig. Then she's over her head in murder when she finds ninety-year-old Mary Hyndman shot to death at her rural upstate farm.

The discovery leaves Deirdre bone-weary and still facing Mary's last request: to deliver a donation to Alsatian House, a Hudson River monastery famous for its German shepherds. Deirdre finds the retreat filled with happy dogs, smiling monks, and peace.

This spur-of-the-moment vacation rejuvenates Deirdre's flagging strength and spirit until another murder tugs on her new leash on life. Deirdre's investigative skills tell her this death is linked to Mary's. But getting her teeth into this case may prove too tough for even a dauntless D.V.M. . . . when a killer with feral instincts brings her a hairsbreadth from death.

DR. NIGHTINGALE GOES THE DISTANCE

Intending to forget about her sick cats and ailing cows for one night, Deirdre "Didi" Quinn Nightingale, D.V.M., is all dressed up for a champagne-sipping prerace gala at a posh thoroughbred farm. She never expects death to be on the guest list while hobnobbing with the horsey set and waiting to meet the famous equine vet, Sam Hull. But when two shots ring out, two bodies lie in the stall of the year's most promising filly.

The renowned Dr. Hull is beyond help, and the filly's distraught owner offers Didi a fee and a thoroughbred all her own to find this killer. Now Deirdre is off snooping in a world of bloodlines, blood money, and bloody schemes. The odds are against this spunky vet, who may find her heart's desire at stake—and murder waiting at the finish line. . . .

DR. NIGHTINGALE ENTERS THE BEAR CAVE

Veterinarian Deirdre "Didi" Nightingale is happily taking a break from her practice to join a research team tagging pregnant black bears in the northern Catskills. Awaiting her are the thrill of adventure, the fun of taking her friend Rose along—and murder.

No sooner do she and Rose arrive at the base camp than they run into the bullet-riddled body of the caretaker. Although local police insist the murder has nothing to do with the scientific expedition, Deirdre feels something fishy is afoot in bear country. She soon finds the paw print of a monster-size bruin, a creature that is a Catskill legend—and a growing reason to suspect one of her group is a killer. Meanwhile, the woods are lovely, dark, and deep. And, for a vet on the trail of a murderer, most deadly.